T0274946

Race Against Time

Corporal Race Monro, an ex-Confederate officer, now a member of the North West Mounted Police, is on a mission into Montana Territory when he is murderously attacked and left for dead by a fellow mounted policeman. But Race survives and has to complete his mission and also bring the murderer to justice.

Race Against Time

P.J. Gallagher

A Black Horse Western

ROBERT HALE

© P.J. Gallagher 2020
First published in Great Britain in 2020

ISBN 978-0-7198-3135-5

The Crowood Press
The Stable Block
Crowood Lane
Ramsbury
Marlborough
Wiltshire SN8 2HR

www.bhwesterns.com

Robert Hale is an imprint
of The Crowood Press

*Dedicated to Swallowfork, aka John Simpson, and
Two Draws, aka Jim Brown, my two pals who introduced
me to Cowboy Action Shooting*

Typeset by
Simon and Sons ITES Services Pvt Ltd
Printed and bound in Great Britain by
4Bind Ltd, Stevenage, SG1 2XT

CHAPTER ONE

Race Munro very slowly regained consciousness, his mind fighting against the physical desire just to let oblivion take over and allow him to relapse into a deep, everlasting sleep. The drum beating inside his head continued its thump, thump, thump against his skull as he reluctantly opened his eyes, wincing at the overhead sunlight, which prompted him to immediately shut them once more.

More cautiously he opened his eyes again and licked his dry, cracked lips; endeavouring to ignore the nauseous sensation that urged him to be sick with every movement, he raised his right hand up to his head in an effort to discover where the pounding was coming from. After an unsatisfactory examination Race lowered his hand and looked at his red fingers with an almost detached interest.

'Hmm,' he thought. 'That's curious! I don't remember having an accident.' He lay quietly for a while with eyes closed, pondering the situation. He had been on some kind of journey – well, a mission more than a mere journey, and he had not been alone. There had been others. Had they had the same accident?

After a while Race reluctantly opened his eyes wide, painfully raised his head and looked around. He was lying on his back, and just beyond his bare feet a campfire was still smouldering. An idle thought entered his mind: 'That's strange, where are my boots?'

He turned his head to the left, wincing as a sharp pain shot across his head with the unwelcome movement. There among the trees the horses had been tethered but not hobbled, since it had not been determined to have an overnight camp at that spot. Somehow, indistinctly, Race remembered that he was the one who had made that judgment. But where were the others?

He turned his head to the right, forcing himself to ignore the pain created by the sudden movement. There, five or six feet away, was one answer to his recent self-question: Kurt Vogel of the blonde hair and Germanic mannerisms, lay on his face, both hands outstretched clutching at handfuls of the sandy soil, and with a huge blackened stain between his shoulder blades where he had been shot in the back.

So that accounted for the second member of their party – but where was the third? Where was Bill Westerman? In age Bill was the senior member of the trio, but in rank the most junior. Race moistened his lips and attempted to call out. Initially all he achieved was a croak, which was answered mockingly by a 'Caw, caw!' from a crow in a nearby tree. He tried again, and eventually succeeded in emitting the word 'Bill!' in a feeble shout. His cry was answered by silence. It was painfully obvious that Bill Westerman was not within hearing distance.

Race sat up, fighting to overcome the pain that his new movement produced, and again looked round for all the customary scenes produced by a campsite. Where were the three saddles that had been taken off to ease the horses' backs? Where was the pack load that he distinctly recalled being placed at the foot of that towering pine? Where was his carbine, which, as was his custom, had been placed close at hand on his left side? And where were his damned boots?

There was a stream immediately in front of him and not too far away. Race licked his dry lips. Could he get that far and get to sip some of the life-giving fluid? He tried to stand but found that his legs just buckled beneath him, so on hands and knees he crawled slowly, and with frequent rests, over to the small creek.

After resting a while he dipped his right hand down into the water and, rolling over, splashed some on his face; then using his palm as an improvised cup he drank, again and again. When he felt refreshed after drinking, he crawled forwards a little, then lowered his head and bathed the wounded side, washing away as best as he could the blood from his matted hair.

7

He examined the furrow about an inch above his right ear. Since it was very obvious that Kurt Vogel had been shot from behind, it seemed fairly obvious that the shot intended for him had also come from the same direction. He would have to investigate – but first he would have to find out what had happened to Bill. With this the last conscious thought in his mind, Race Munro, exhausted by his recent efforts, fell into a troubled half sleep.

***

He was awoken by his head being moved as something soft was placed under it, and with relief, Race inquired: 'Bill! Are you OK?' followed by, 'What happened to you?'

A cracked gravelly voice, which was certainly not that of Bill Westerman, responded to his query: 'Well, sonny, I sure ain't Bill, whoever he might be. Fred Turner is the name. Always has bin for nigh on eighty years, but you can call me Alfie if it pleases you. You've had one nasty crack on the head an' you're lucky to still be in the land of the living, so you just rest easy now while I do some field first aid on that wound of yourn.'

Race lay quietly while the stranger – what did he say his name was? Fred something or other – ministered to his aching head. He felt it being washed tenderly, then dried, and the wound dressed with some kind of paste or ointment before being wrapped round and around with cloth as in a turban. During these proceedings Race was content to lie motionless while the stranger gently administered his medical skills – and once again he fell asleep.

It must have been hours later that he awoke, quickly aware of being far more conscious of his surroundings. When he opened his eyes he saw that he was now wrapped in a blanket, and putting a hand to his head, noted that it was covered with swathes of cloth. Several feet away he perceived a stranger doing something over a small fire, but also looking towards him with concern. Noting the interest that Race displayed, the stranger rose to his feet and crossed over to where Race lay: looking down, a smile appeared on his leathery whiskered features.

'Howdy young fella! I see that you've decided to join me in the land of the living. Well, I hope you enjoyed your beauty sleep! You were out long enough.'

Race took a long moment to digest this information, and then asked the stranger's name, but apologizing: 'I believe you told me who you are, but I'm sorry, I just can't remember.'

The stranger smiled, and remarked that with a wound of the type that Race had experienced he was bound to be a trifle vague about the event. He then went on to introduce himself.

'My name is Fred Turner, but most people call me Alfie. I was just riding by when Jethro – that's my mule, by the way – decided that he wanted a drink and turned off the trail to this little creek here. That's when I found you and the other poor fella. You'd both been dry-gulched from over there,' he indicated a location about seventy-five yards away dominated by a huge pine tree.

'I found two shell cases over there. Both had been recently fired. I brought them over in case you wanted to see them. Perhaps it could give you an idea as to who would have wanted you and your buddy out of the way.'

Alfie Turner handed Race two brass rifle cases. He recognized them immediately, but to make sure, he turned them so that he could read the inscription on the base: .577 Snider, Eley. He turned the Snider cases over and over in his hand, while all sorts of wild thoughts tumbled through his mind. He was tempted to blurt out his suspicions to Alfie, but decided that for the moment he would just tell him the bare truth.

'I and my two buddies were on the way to Fort Benson, and one of us suggested that we stop here and rest the horses and brew up some coffee before continuing with our journey. It's a good job there was a doctor in the area!' here Race ruefully tapped the side of his bandaged head.

Alfie looked at him in embarrassment. 'Son, I ain't no sawbones. I just have a way with animals, and go from place to place making their little lives a wee bit better. I figured that treating your gunshot would be no different than working on any other animal that had got tore up in some way. No offence intended.'

Race shook his head and instantly regretted doing so. 'No offence taken, old-timer, I'm beholden to you!'

'Say, young fella! You say there were three of you going to Fort Benson. Well, you're here, and that poor lad is over there…' – he pointed to where Kurt's body lay under a piece of tarp – '…but where's your third friend? Maybe there's another body around here somewhere?'

Race struggled to his feet, but swayed and would have fallen if Alfie Turner hadn't grabbed him by the elbow. 'Steady lad! You sit down and rest awhile! I'll scout around a bit and see if I can find any sign of your missing partner!'

CHAPTER TWO

Off he went, searching the whole area in ever-increasing circles with nothing escaping those sharp old eyes of his, while Race sat and pondered the circumstances that had brought him to this place.

He had been born on one of the sea islands south of Savannah, Georgia, where his father eked out a living as a teacher to the sons of the local gentry. It was because of his father's love of the classics that he was burdened with the name Horace, which from childhood he detested and shortened at the first opportunity

When he was in his late teens, Georgians took part in the fight for Southern independence, and Race became an infantry officer in the Fourth Georgia Rifles. And as history records, the South lost the war. Strangely Captain Race Munro had not been in the country when General Lee surrendered at Appomattox. Race, along with several other Confederate officers, had been sent up into Canada to organize raids down into New York and other northern states. When hostilities ended he had been warned that the Federal Government was intent on making life difficult for Johnny Rebs who had operated from Canada, and therefore he had remained in exile.

The years had passed away and Race had found varied employment, mostly in Ontario where he remained in loose contact with other Southern sympathizers. He was not too unhappy. He had work, he had money in his pockets and he had friends. He detested the Canadian winters, but then so did most people, and gradually his accent had modified itself so that he no longer used colloquialisms in nearly every sentence.

The one thing that he did miss was the excitement of the war years and the military life, even with all its hardships. It was therefore of great interest in May of 1873 that he read that Sir John A. MacDonald, the prime minister, was intent on raising a force of mounted police to patrol the far western plains of Canada. Race made further inquiries and eventually enlisted in the new force, which was to be known as the North West Mounted Police, NWMP.

On 8 July 1874 Race, clad in scarlet tunic, blue pants with a yellow stripe down each leg and wearing a blue pillbox hat, together with 275 other similarly dressed men under Commissioner George Arthur French, marched west from Fort Dufferin, Manitoba. Each man was armed with a .577 Snider carbine and a .45 Caliber Adams revolver, and in addition the column had two 9-pounder cannon.

Their tasks, among several, were to break up the inter-tribal warfare between the Blackfoot and the Crow Indians, and stop the flow of illegal liquor that was destroying the tribes. The whiskey traders were known to be operating from several illicit forts, the most infamous being Fort Whoop-up, where they dispensed a noxious brew called 'frontier whiskey', made up from a quart of whiskey, a pound of chewing tobacco, a handful of red peppers, one bottle of Jamaican ginger, a quart of molasses and a dash of red ink. The effect of this concoction was said to be stunning.

The column was short of wood, water and other essentials. Water holes used by buffalo for wallows produced an evil-smelling liquid that was black in colour, but which was all the men had to drink. An encounter with a wandering band of Sioux Indians left a lasting impression. Every man in the column, from the Commissioner down, was infested with fleas and lice.

Colonel French decided to take a party with wagons across the border to Fort Benson. There he could obtain much needed supplies and obtain news from Ottawa. He sent for Corporal Race Munro. The military training that the latter had received had not gone unnoticed by the colonel, and Race's promotion from trooper to corporal had come quite early in his police career. These were Colonel French's orders:

'Munro, I am taking a party to obtain supplies from Fort Benson, which I understand is just over the border. I want you, with a suitable escort, to form an advance party, get to Benson, arrange for the purchase of supplies, and have them ready for when I arrive with the wagons.

'Here is a list of foodstuffs which I think should be available, and here is a letter of credit, which you may draw upon to pay for the products. I know that you, um ah, had problems due to the civil strife but that's all over now and I have complete trust in you. Now choose the two men to accompany you. Draw rations and prepare to start as soon as is possible. You will all have to wear civilian clothing since you are out of Canada but take your small arms with you. I think you may find most Americans carry a gun so that won't be out of place.'

Race had saluted and left the headquarters' tent with his head in a whirl. He went first to the commissariat area, where he arranged for a week's rations for three to be made up, and then to his troop lines, pondering the while as to whom he should select to accompany him. After much thought he decided to take troopers Vogel and Westerman. The experience would certainly help the young German trooper to gain confidence in his own abilities, as to date, he often relied upon others in the troop. Westerman, an ex-Union army soldier, was older than most and sometimes appeared to have a chip on his shoulder. He was a handsome man, above normal height, who would have been extremely good looking were it not for a knife scar from below the left eye down to the chin. But generally they had both appeared steady men, and were not among the grumblers who recently tended to be in the majority.

Race had called them to one side and informed them of the task, telling them of the journey and of the purpose. He had then indicated that the choice was up to them: if they wanted to go they had to volunteer – he would not order them to accompany him.

Both men had indicated their eagerness to be part of the party, and both had pressed him for more details about the nature of their task. Race had explained patiently that they had to buy large quantities of food to provide for the whole column, and young Vogel had commented that surely that would take a lot of money – to which Race had replied something to the effect that money was no problem for them.

They had left the column, three riders and a pack horse, and headed south-west into the American state of Montana. All went well. The weather remained acceptable, sunny during the daytime and cold at night. The trees were beginning to turn, telling the world that winter was approaching, though hopefully still a long way off.

Kurt Vogel was full of chatter, obviously proud that he had been given such a chance to prove himself. By comparison, Bill Westerman had little to say, seeming preoccupied most of the time, but certainly pulling his weight whenever there was work to be done when setting up camp. As they went deeper into American territory Race reflected that it was being a pleasant journey, almost like a holiday.

CHAPTER THREE

Race's reverie over the recent and not-so-recent events leading up to the shooting was brought to a sudden halt and a return to the present by a loud shout from Alfie Turner: 'Hey, lad! Look what I've found!'

Race sat up and turned his head in the direction of the voice. Alfie was coming through the trees triumphantly waving a pair of boots. He approached, and Race was disappointed to see that the footwear carried by the old man was not his pair of cherished military boots, but an old, cracked, unpolished pair that had been worn until recently by one Trooper Bill Westerman. But why had Bill thrown away his boots?

Still befuddled by the shot that had nearly ended his earthly existence, Race sat silently staring from the pair of boots placed before him to the two Snider cartridge cases he held in his left hand. The awful implication of both boots and shell cases exploded into his train of thought, and initially he rejected it.

'Bill Westerman shot Kurt and attempted to kill me!' Slowly the cold logic of the situation impressed itself in his mind, and he was faced with the fact that a comrade and fellow trooper had wilfully tried to murder two fellow policemen. But why?

Alfie Turner stood by silently while Race pondered the situation, then, when the latter made no comment, he volunteered the information that he'd found, along with the boots, two saddlebags, both of which had been thoroughly ransacked.

Race grimaced as his aching head slowly digested the latest information, and he slowly reasoned out what had actually happened. Bill had deliberately shot both him and Kurt. But why? For the boots that he had stolen? No! There had to be something far more than that. He thought back, and at length realized that the one topic that had come up at irregular intervals was the high cost of the supplies they had to buy at Fort Benson. He recalled Westerman saying on more than one occasion, 'Them supplies is sure gonna cost an awful lot of money!' And he had replied, 'They sure are, Bill!' but without any further comment.

Gradually, Race came to accept that Bill Westerman had thought that he, Race, had on his person, or in his saddlebags, a large sum of money with which to buy the supplies needed by the column. He must have been driven to distraction when, having done the awful deed, he searched the saddlebags and found no money.

Race felt for the inside pocket of the civilian jacket that he was wearing and retrieved the envelope given to him by Colonel French. All was intact: the list of supplies needed, the line of credit, and a letter to the American commandant at Fort Benson. He decided that it was time to tell Alfie Turner the whole story, and therefore proceeded to do so.

When he had completed his story he sat there silently staring off into space while Alfie Turner digested the information that he had been given. Finally he spoke: 'So, Corporal Munro! Is that correct? You've got to get to Fort Benson as fast as possible and you ain't got no horse. How are you going to do that?'

Race looked up at the old-timer and shook his head as he shrugged his shoulders in despair. In his wounded state he just couldn't think dispassionately and develop a logical course of action. Alfie came to his rescue. 'I'm going to finish fixing us some supper and then you are going to sleep. In fact, if you want to sleep while I'm getting organized, you go right ahead.

'In the morning, after a good sleep, I'll introduce you to Jethro. He's just a mule, but he's an honest mule and I'll loan him to you to get to Fort Benson. Leave him at the fort. He'll be OK there. They know him. I'll just take my own time and get there eventually. Now, I'll leave you to rest while I fix the grub.'

After a restless night's sleep Race awoke and looked around. Old Alf was already up and the coffee pot was on the fire along with a pan containing bacon and beans. Race hurriedly splashed some water from the nearby stream on to his face in lieu of a morning wash, and at Alf's bidding sat down and did fair justice to the breakfast prepared for him.

After the meal Alfie examined Race's wound and replaced the bandages with a large piece of sticky plaster, remarking that he used the same treatment on a horse's legs if they had a bad cut from that new-fangled barbed wire that was appearing in the West.

He then rummaged in his pack and finally produced a percussion .36 caliber Colt revolver, which he proceeded to load and cap before replacing it in a home-made leather holster. He then handed the rig to Race.

'Here you are, Corporal. I figure you should have some means of protection while you're travelling to Fort Benson. Now I know this is an old-fashioned muzzle-loading weapon by today's standards, but there's still a great many men using them effectively – including, I might add, one James Butler Hickok – so it should serve the purpose.'

In vain Race protested that he couldn't take the old man's means of defense. Alfie was insistent, 'No, lad, I'll be perfectly safe. I'm well known in these parts, and if someone attacks me, well, first he wouldn't get any money as I don't carry any, and secondly, he'd be depriving the local folks of an animal doctor, and that wouldn't go down well. No, you take the pistol, and welcome to it. Now come on, I'll introduce you to Jethro!'

Race took the holstered pistol and strapped it on, putting the box of paper cartridges and a circular tin containing percussion caps in the left pocket of his jacket before following Alfie across the clearing to where Jethro the mule was patiently browsing on the lower foliage.

Introductions were solemnly made, although Jethro did not seem particularly interested. Alfie had brought the two saddlebags belonging to Race and secured them behind Jethro's McClellan saddle, along with a small sack containing bacon, beans and a number of corn dodgers. Alfie apologized for the lack of utensils, but produced a metal lid in which Race could heat up some vittles.

'You'll have to make do with water for drinking. We had the last of the coffee this morning. Now off you go, lad, and take care of old Jethro.'

Race climbed into the saddle and, settling himself down, urged Jethro forwards. The mule didn't move. Race tried again. Jethro looked round at his rider and smiled contemptuously, it seemed, showing his big yellow teeth before resuming eating the foliage. Race looked down at Alfie in bewilderment. 'What do I need to do to get this critter moving?'

Alfie went over to the bushes and cut off a limb, carefully trimming off the smaller branches before handing the switch to Race. 'Jethro needs a starter to get him in the travelling mood. This should do the trick. Just lay this on his rear quarters a few times and he'll accept that you mean business!'

21

Race did as advised, and Jethro immediately ceased munching – ignoring his master, he broke into a shambling trot, which Race found uncomfortable compared to the gait of his stolen horse, but which did eat up the miles.

Waving to Alfie, Race left the clearing and headed south-west on a well defined trail, which he had been assured would take him eventually to Fort Benson.

CHAPTER FOUR

Race's first day on the trail was, in the main, uneventful. He rode through rolling hill country dotted with areas of woodland and brush-filled gullies, from which on several occasions white-tailed deer would start up in fright if they were grazing too close to the trail. It wasn't until mid-afternoon that he encountered any other travellers, and they consisted of an Indian clad in cast-off white man's attire, his squaw wearing an old tattered dress, and two half-naked children.

The children ran alongside with their hands held out in the universal supplication for begging, which caused the man he supposed to be their father to speak sharply to them, while he said something in an apologetic manner and shrugged his shoulders as though to say; 'Sorry, they are kids. They mean no harm!'

Race dug in his pants pocket and extracted some small Canadian coins, which he tossed down to the children, saying to the Indian: 'They're nice kids. Buy them some candy. That's Canadian money, but you should be able to use it, especially near to the border.'

He applied his switch, causing Jethro to quicken his pace, leaving the impoverished Indian family behind. 'Now what prompted me to give handouts to a couple of begging children? I've got enough problems of my own without becoming the local philanthropist.' Race shook his head, pondering over his sudden generosity, and mentally resolving to be more dispassionate in the future, he started looking for a suitable choice for a lonely overnight camp.

On the second day he met up with more travellers proceeding in both directions. Most greeted him with a typical: 'Howdy stranger!' and exchanged the usual observations regarding the weather, the state of the trail and so forth, while a couple broke the Golden Rule of the West by asking him where he was coming from and also where he was going.

Several noted from his garb that he was a stranger in those parts, and took him for an Englishman because of the cut of his whipcord riding breeches, Norfolk jacket and shallow-brimmed hat. Their observations caused Race to consider that, if he was going to hunt down Bill Westerman, then he might have to obtain clothing more applicable to the American West so that he was less conspicuous.

The following day, as Race neared Fort Benson, his mode of dress was the major factor in a confrontation that occurred between himself and two local hooligans. About two miles from the fort, Race was entering an area which, although not fully urbanized, had more than a scattering of sod-roofed huts and similar buildings. Jethro was just ambling along, and Race was content to let the mule set the pace since they were reaching the end of their travels together. For some reason the sight of the differently dressed stranger, perched on the old grey mule, was a source of merriment to the two young men lounging on a seat to the right of the road.

Not content just with the sight that they found so amusing, the two started catcalling and shouting out derogatory remarks designed to embarrass the rider and draw him to the attention of others.

'Hey, Fancy Pants! Hey, Limey! Did you lose your way?' and a barrage of other comments and obscene remarks followed, each more unpleasant than anything they had uttered earlier. Race made no response, but merely looked ahead and tried to ignore them.

Unfortunately that just annoyed them more, and the pair started picking up clods of earth and stones, tossing them in his general direction. Race had had enough. He was wearing the pistol, given to him by Alfie, on his left side and it was therefore hidden from the two yahoos, who no doubt thought that the stranger was unarmed – so when their victim suddenly swung around in the saddle and pointed a large-calibre cocked revolver at them, they were terrified!

'Listen, you obnoxious, ill-favoured bastards! If you don't run away and find somewhere else to play, I'm gonna gut shoot the pair of you. It'll be self defence since you've chosen to attack me, so you've got a choice: persist in your bad behaviour and die, or go home and probably live to an old age. What is it to be?' And Race fired a single shot that removed the hat from the taller of the two rapscallions.

For one frozen moment of time the pair stared at each other, while the grim-faced rider unwaveringly pointed his revolver at them, a weapon that seemed to grow in size with every second that passed. The two now terrified hooligans stood as though petrified, with mouths gaping open, convinced that they were facing their last moments on earth. Race gestured with the muzzle of his pistol, indicating for them to go – and not waiting to retrieve the hat from the ground, the two took off as though running in a foot race, and rapidly disappeared amid the shanties.

Race holstered his pistol and resumed his journey, with no further experiences until he reached Fort Benson. The fort had originally been constructed by a fur trading company as a typical Western-style, stockaded fortification, with tree trunks lashed together vertically for walls, and with corner towers and a gatehouse constructed using the same local material. Later, however, it had been rebuilt using adobe brick, as this material was considered to be more durable. At the time of Race's visit it had become a military establishment, due to the restless nature of the surrounding tribes. As was normal during the day and in peacetime conditions, the main gate was wide open, with the entry guarded by a solitary soldier in blue uniform.

CHAPTER FIVE

Despite an inward tensing on Race's part upon facing his first man in the uniform of the victors of the Civil War, he assumed a nonchalant air as he rode towards the gateway. As was to be expected, he was challenged by the sentry: 'Halt! Who goes there! State your name and your business!'

'Munro is the name, of the Canadian North West Mounted Police. I have a letter to be presented to the commandant of Fort Benson.'

The sentry saluted and indicated a building on the far side of the parade ground, directly behind the flag pole flanked by two light cannon. As Race lightly switched Jethro's withers to urge him to make this last little journey, the guard exclaimed: 'Say! Ain't that Jethro, old Alfie Turner's mule? Where's Alfie?'

Indicating that his queries would be answered in due course, Race rode across the parade ground, past the flag that he had rejected, and reined up at a hitching rail in front of a building marked HQ. Another sentry was standing at ease by the doorway of the HQ, and as Race dismounted, the former called into the interior of the building: 'Sarge, you've got a visitor!' With that remark, a burly blue-uniformed figure with the insignia of a master sergeant appeared and stood in the doorway, hands on hips, as Race mounted the steps and approached.

'Good afternoon, Sergeant! The name is Munro, corporal of the North West Mounted Police of Canada. I have an urgent letter for your commandant.'

The large non-com held out his hand for the letter, but Race shook his head. 'Sorry, Sergeant! This has to be handed personally to the commandant himself. So if I may see him, please!'

The orderly sergeant, O'Hara by name, huffed and muttered something about regulations, but finally relented and escorted Race forwards to an inner office, where, after knocking and receiving permission to enter, he went in and announced that a foreign soldier was requesting an interview with Major Carson. Major Carson was apparently agreeable, since O'Hara returned to the outer office immediately and stated curtly that Race might go in.

Race did so, and approached the large desk where a uniformed figure was seated, bent over a mass of papers; he halted in the best drill-ground manner of the British Army as practised by the NWMP, and saluted smartly. The head-bent figure looked up, and there was a mutually shocked reaction on the part of both men: 'Good God! It's Horace Munro! Where did you spring from?' The commandant jumped up from his chair and seized Munro's right hand, and started shaking it up and down violently.

Race responded in a like manner, grasping the major's left arm at the elbow while shaking hands with him with equal vigour while they stood grinning at each other. Finally Race declared: 'Archibald Carson, by all the powers! Commandant of Fort Benson and a major to boot! Well, if that doesn't beat the band!'

He would have continued, but Major Carson hurriedly interjected: '*Archie* Carson please, *not* Archibald – any more than you like being called Horace, as I recall! It's Race, isn't it? And what's all this about you being a Canadian policeman? Sit down and tell me all about yourself!'

Race took a chair from the wall and placed it close to the desk, while the other went and carefully closed the door; as he returned he placed one finger to his lips before seating himself and saying quietly: 'One can never be too careful, even on an army post! Now, tell me all about yourself, and what brings you here?'

Race took a deep breath and then launched into a detailed account, describing how, when the split occurred between north and south, he had felt duty bound to leave West Point and return to Georgia, where he had offered his services to the Confederate government at Richmond. He related how he had served in various capacities, finally being sent up to Canada, and how he was in Ontario when the war ended.

'You know, Archie, many of us Johnny Rebs were treated pretty badly by the majority of Union officials,

29

so we remained as exiles. I eventually became a Canadian citizen, and when the North West Mounted Police was formed I enlisted as a trooper.' Here he reached into an inner pocket of his jacket and produced the letter from Colonel French, which he passed to Major Carson.

Carson scanned the letter rapidly, remarking that he had been expecting such a missive, as he had been instructed from Washington to render such aid as was required by the Canadians. Then glancing out of his window towards the parade ground he enquired: 'But Race! How come you have arrived on old Jethro, Alfie Turner's mule?'

Race gave him a short, terse account of the events that had befallen them, from the time they had crossed the border, describing the shooting as he remembered it, and showing his friend his plastered head.

'Now, Archie, what I want from you is assistance in getting this list of supplies filled using the letter of credit that Colonel French has given me, and assistance in re-equipping myself so that I can go after this Bill Westerman. I need American civilian clothing, a horse – or better still, two horses so I can use one as a pack animal – and firearms. Can you help me?'

Archie Carson pursed his lips and mulled over the questions: 'Well, Race, the stores are no problem – I'll get my quartermaster sergeant working on those right away. He has a good relationship with the local stores, and can no doubt obtain everything that

Colonel French requires. Equally, our sutler's store here in the fort can no doubt sell you all the clothing that you require, and possibly all the firearms. If not, there is a gunsmith in town who would carry what you need.

'However, having said that, Race, there is a problem. You are now an alien in the United States and have no legal standing under which you can pursue and capture or kill this miscreant, who no doubt deserves punishment. I can't even swear you in as a deputy US marshal, because in doing so you would have to pledge loyalty to Washington, and you have renounced that by becoming a Canadian and therefore a British subject.'

Carson grinned at Race, and continued: 'But let's cross that bridge later. The first thing is to get those supplies ready. O'Hara!'

The orderly sergeant entered with a crash of boots, and Major Carson had him seek out the quartermaster from his cubbyhole and start working on the list of supplies. In addition he instructed O'Hara to have someone unsaddle Jethro and turn the mule loose. Having advanced a reasonable sum in American dollars drawn against the line of credit given to Race by Colonel French, Archie Carson suggested that they walk over to the sutler's store to see if he had any suitable clothing in stock.

It was as though the Civil War had never separated these two West Point friends. Walking across the parade ground they talked animatedly about mutual friends and the years that had divided them, although both tried to skirt round the issues that had divided north and south.

At the sutler's store Race purchased a pair of jeans, a check wool shirt, and a canvas vest similar to those worn by most of the civilians that he had encountered. After advice, he picked up a blue duffle coat to wear should the weather turn inclement, and a brown sombrero – and seeing some footwear, he thankfully exchanged the old boots that Westerman had discarded when he had stolen those belonging to Race, and picked up a pair of nearly new cavalry ones, which seemed very comfortable.

The sutler had but a limited number of handguns for sale, none of which impressed Race with either their model or condition, and Major Carson suggested that a visit to the gunsmith in town might prove profitable. Two army mounts were provided, and Major Carson accompanied Race on the visit to the purveyor of firearms in the Benson area of Montana.

Halfway down the dusty unpaved street that represented the down-town area of Benson was a store with an over-sized outline of a long gun above a swinging sign stating 'Guns' and in smaller print J. Schultz, Proprietor: they had arrived at their destination. Dismounting and securing their horses at the hitching rail, they mounted the steps to the crude boardwalk and entered the store.

Race looked around with interest as Archie Carson greeted the bald-headed bespectacled man standing expectantly behind the counter, 'Hello, John! I've brought you a customer. This is my good friend Race Munro. He's looking to buy a good revolver. What have you got in stock?'

John Schultz wiped his hands on his apron and thrust out his right arm. 'Howdy Mister Munro. Vot kind of handgun do you vant?'

Race, thinking of his Mounted Police revolver stolen by Westerman, indicated that he preferred a large-calibre pistol – at which point Schultz raised his hand to interrupt him, and reaching under the counter, produced a rectangular cardboard case.

'Mister Munro, what I haf here is de latest Colt model! Dis is the new Colt revolver – the Artillery model mit a seven and a half inch long barrel in .45 calibre! Dey only came out last year, and dis is the first one I haf!'

Slowly and almost ceremoniously he opened the case to reveal a gleaming revolver with a deep blue finish and polished walnut grips.

Race took up the piece, noting subconsciously the way it fitted into his hand, and how well balanced it was as he held it out and sighted along the barrel. He opened the loading gate and closed it, squeezing the action as he did so. Nothing happened. He looked at Schultz, puzzled for a moment, but the gunsmith took the piece from him and said, 'Single action, Mister Munro. You must cock de piece first!'

He handed the revolver back to Race, who did as instructed. The well-tuned action clicked as he cocked it and squeezed the trigger, which dropped the hammer with a loud sound. Race was satisfied.

'Very good, Mr Schultz, I would like to purchase this revolver if I may, and I think that I should take perhaps one hundred and fifty cartridges for it, if you have that many available.'

He looked around, considering what other items he might require, and seeing a cartridge belt and open holster hanging up, added those to his purchases. Then the thought that he might need to engage in a long-distance dual with the missing Westerman drew his attention to the long guns racked against the far wall, and he wandered over to look at them with interest.

He was startled to notice among them two Snider carbines, and reaching out, picked one up with the intention of examining it. Then he was overcome with a mixture of emotions, and declared:

'Mr Schultz, where did you get these Sniders? This one I'm holding in my hands is my own, stolen from me by a murdering, duplicitous individual whom I am determined to bring to justice!'

John Schultz stared at Race, then at Archie Carson, and back to Race. 'But gentlemen, you must understand! I did not know these things. Several days ago a man he comes into my store. He has two Sniders to sell. He tells me that he won dem in a crap game across de border.' He appealed to Major Carson. 'You must understand, Major! I believed dat man. I think he tells me the truth!'

34

Both Archie Carson and Race Munro hastened to assure the crestfallen gunsmith that he was not under any suspicion, and it was arranged that he would receive a nominal sum for surrendering the two Sniders over to the care of the US Army. Realizing that he would not be too far out of pocket over them, Schultz hastened to complete the sale of the Colt, the belt and holster, and the ammunition, not only in .45 calibre, but also a box of hefty .577 Snider cartridges that he happened to have in stock.

The two friends returned to Fort Benson, where in the privacy of Major Carson's office, Race changed into the clothing that he'd bought at the sutler's store.

Alfie Turner's old muzzle-loading Colt in its home-made holster was solemnly handed over to Archie Carson, to be returned to its original owner. Then with the new Colt slung on his left side, and a belt whose loops were filled with shiny brass cartridges, Race donned the sombrero and posed for approval before Archie Carson: 'Well, Archie! Will I pass as a local?'

Major Carson looked at him critically, and after a moment's silence shook his head. 'No, Race. You look like a dude. An Easterner pretending to be a man of the West! Here!' He took Race's hat and proceeded to kick it around the room until it presented a rather worn, battered appearance.

'There, that's a start. Now, if we can create the same look with the rest of your duds, maybe you'll pass.

Take your gun-belt off and roll around in the dust a while – that should remove some of your newness.'

Race did as he was advised, and eventually received Carson's grudging approval: 'Well, you'll do if people don't look too closely! Now, to more serious business. Your legal capacity!

'We agreed that you can't be a temporary US marshal because of the oath, and the fact that you are an alien, having renounced your American citizenship. However, I think there is another office that will give you some legal standing. You could be a temporary Assistant Marshal of Montana. In this case you would merely swear an oath to uphold the laws of the Territory of Montana. It would also give you some quasi-legality beyond the state border. What do you think?'

Race, eager to be on the trail of the murderous NWMP deserter, agreed; after a brief ceremony he was sworn in as a Montana marshal, and was presented with a small shield engraved with the word 'Marshal', which he pinned on his left breast pocket.

CHAPTER SIX

A day later Race left Fort Benson riding a large sorrel gelding purchased from the US Army. His clothing looked scuffed and worn. In his saddlebags were the few personal items that he considered essential, while following docilely behind was a small grey mare serving as a pack animal, laden with basic camping equipment to afford Race independence on the trail.

Even with such limited time he had managed to get in an hour's practice with the Colt revolver that he had purchased. He was immediately impressed by the smooth action, and especially the way that the pistol rolled upwards, absorbing the recoil as he fired – so different from the butt shape of the Adams .45 with which he was familiar.

Race and Archie Carson had spent the previous evening attempting to rough out a basic plan of action. From the information provided by John Schultz, Westerman had been in Fort Benson six days ago and had then apparently vanished. Inquiries in town merely revealed that he had bought some basic trail fodder, presumably with the money he obtained by selling the two Snider carbines. He had patronized one of the two saloons in town, but had just had two beers on each occasion and had not socialized. Nobody remembered seeing him leave town. In fact most people could not remember him well enough to provide a decent description of the man. Now, where would he have headed?

It was surmised that he would have gone south to get away from the border, where there was always the possibility of being discovered by some traveller from Canada. But all this was purely speculation.

As he rode south from Fort Benson, Race thought to himself that since he didn't have even the slightest clue as to Westerman's whereabouts, was he in fact going on a wild goose chase? Time would tell.

Another factor that Race had to consider seriously was the weather. It was now the fall, trees were beginning to lose their foliage, and the first snowfall could occur at any time. Folks in Fort Benson said that, hopefully, there would be an Indian summer, that period of mild warm weather that often developed after the first frost. Race prayed that such would be the case, as it would certainly make life easier for him.

As Race proceeded south he stopped and inquired of everyone he saw as to whether anyone had seen a tall scarred stranger passing that way recently. There were no positive replies, and it would seem that Westerman had vanished into thin air.

He stopped and chatted to an elderly man splitting logs for firewood. He was quite happy to rest from his labours. He did not recall any scarred strangers, but did remember a brownish grey mare with a white blaze running down its face. Race was heartened by this news, as such a description could tally with that of the fugitive. He rode on, elated by the first clue as to Westerman's whereabouts.

About an hour later, on a lonely section of the trail where the trees on both sides came down to the roadside, he heard noises and pulled gently on the reins to bring the sorrel to a halt. Off to the right the ground fell away gently to an open clearing surrounded by trees. From the clearing came cries of coarse laughter amid whoops and yells of 'yeehaw', along with higher-pitched screams of fear and a woman pleading in an unknown tongue.

CHAPTER SEVEN

Race tied the grey mare to a convenient shrub and eased the sorrel down the slope between the trees to the clearing. As he approached, the details of the uproar became clear. Sitting cross-legged on the ground on a Hudson's Bay blanket was an old man with wrinkled features. His grey-haired head was bowed, then from time to time he would raise both hands and simultaneously look up into the sky while his lips moved in prayer. He seemed oblivious of the mayhem going on around him, as half-a-dozen white-skinned louts strode about, wrecking the Indians' camp, opening bags and tossing the contents about, and giggling maliciously at their own antics. Two, after a dispute of some kind, mounted their horses and rode to and fro across the clearing, trampling the natives' possessions beneath the hooves of their steeds, while an older woman and a much younger one cried for them to stop.

Race had seen enough. Not merely because of his police training, but every fibre of his being rebelled against the type of bullying these men were perpetrating against helpless people, whatever their skin or race.

Drawing his pistol he rode into the clearing, and pointing the muzzle into the air, fired a single shot. The result was an instantaneous ceasing of all activities – for a moment. The bearded ruffian who had just ripped open the deerskin shirt of the younger woman quickly dropped his hand to his side. The two horsemen reined to a halt, and those on foot stood in open-mouthed surprise at this interruption of their fun.

Before they could respond vocally – no doubt to inquire who this fellow was, breaking up their little bit of innocent pleasure – Race spoke. No – he didn't speak, he roared in a loud, stentorian bellow, which, when drilling NWMP recruits at the depot, had so impressed Colonel French that he had promoted him on the spot.

'You slimy bunch of misbegotten creatures, my name is Munro. Marshal Munro, and I want this campsite cleaned up and all the possessions returned to these people. And if it is not done pronto, I'm going to drag you all down to Fort Benson where you will no doubt spend some time in the hoosegow. Now, *move!*' And he literally screamed the operative order.

Race watched them with narrowed eyes, his pistol moving back and forth as they scurried around repacking the ripped open packs and attempting to bring some kind of order to the mess that they had created.

While the work was in progress one of these yahoos decided that he would try a shot at the marshal, and surreptitiously drew his Remington. He was in the act of aiming it across the back of the horse he was holding when Race saw the hostile movement and fired. The Colt bellowed and the target screamed, clutching at his shoulder as a trail of grey smoke drifted across the clearing and the sound of the solitary shot echoed and re-echoed among the surrounding hills.

Race touched his spurred heels gently to the sorrel and moved forwards. Pointing with his Colt at another of the ruffians, he ordered him to administer first aid to the youth who was wounded, stating: 'You there! Fix up your pal so that he can move out. It's only a flesh wound so don't spend too much time about it. It's either that, or I waste another round putting him out of his misery for disobeying my direct order. Now, *hustle*!' He roared the last word, prompting the one he addressed to run stumbling over to where his fellow stood holding his wounded shoulder and moaning with the pain.

The younger of the two Indian women, having relaced her shirt, came to where Race was supervising the camp clean-up. The older woman watched, eagle-eyed as their possessions were repacked, while the old man ignored the hubbub around him and continued with his prayers.

Race, uncertain as to whether the younger woman understood English, motioned towards the revolver lying by the wounded individual, and addressed her:

'Go. Pick up the gun on the grass and give it to me, please!'

She smiled and hastened to obey, walking over and picking up the gun by the barrel; she handed it to him, saying mischievously; 'Here is white man's little thunder stick!' Then, abandoning the pidgin English, she continued: 'We – that is, my grandfather, my mother and I – are deeply grateful that you intervened in the trouble we were experiencing, and on behalf of my family I thank you!' She ended her little speech by making an elegant curtsy, while Race stared in surprise.

He quickly recovered his composure, and having thanked her, a trifle curtly thrust the pistol into one of his saddlebags. He gathered the group of silent white men together and, after obtaining additional information, issued some terse orders.

He had determined that four of the group were brothers from Zion, a small community close to Great Falls. The other two hailed from the latter town. They had all met up on the trail, and one of the six had produced a jug of 'Frontier Lightning', a particularly potent version of home-made mountain brew. After consuming all the contents of the aforesaid jug, they were seeking any kind of devilment when they came upon the small group of Indians – and the liquor did the talking. Now at least four of the boys were ashamed of their behaviour, and fervently prayed that their father, the Constable of Zion, did not learn of his misdeeds, especially since he 'did not spare the rod' when it came to punishment.

The other two were more hardened characters; they were the only ones to carry firearms, one of which was now in Race's saddle bag.

'OK, you four Zion lads, I'm sending you on your way. You are to go straight home, and I'll check with your father when I'm in that area to ensure that you're all going straight. If you are, I'll not mention this recent episode. So the future is up to you!'

The four brothers expressed fervent thanks for the marshal's decision, and heading to where their horses were tethered, they mounted and took off without bidding farewell to the other two characters. These two stood there half defiantly, one nursing his wounded shoulder, the other with arms folded as though he were framing the words: 'Well, what are you going to do about *us*?'

Race's next move startled and more than a little frightened him, as the 'marshal' suddenly drew his Colt and presented a cocked pistol to them. 'Before we go any further I think I'll just draw your teeth. You with the holstered pistol. Take it out very slowly with just one finger and your thumb, and place it on the ground in front of where you're standing. Then both of you move fifteen paces to your right. Now! Get rid of that gun slowly, move!' and in slow motion the one possessing the revolver did as he was instructed, whereupon Race called upon the Indian girl to pick up the weapon lying on the ground and hand it up to him.

She did so and Race, having put yet another pistol in his saddle bag, holstered his own Colt and prepared to dismount. Afterwards, in reliving what happened, he realized that he took his eyes off the two men for no more than four or five seconds – but it was enough. There was a cry of warning from the Indian girl, and he felt a blow, and instant pain above the left shoulder blade, as the knife hurled by the man he'd just disarmed struck him with a glancing blow, but ripping his flesh as it fell to the ground.

Race reacted swiftly as the would-be murderer reached for yet another blade in his boot, while his fellow drew a stiletto-like knife from where it nestled between his shoulders. He drew his Colt and, thumbing back the hammer, fired at both men coming towards him. The 250-grain lead bullets, driven by forty grains of black powder, stopped both men in their tracks and hurled them lifeless to the ground. Race sank back against the side of his sorrel, sick with the pain in his shoulder, and also sick that his first attempt in Montana to act as a marshal should have had such deadly consequences.

The Indian girl approached: 'I think perhaps you should let me look at your back, Marshal. You're losing a lot of blood.'

Race nodded weakly to her, and holstering his Colt, fumbled with his shirt buttons, his fingers trembling in reaction to the recent attack. He attempted to pull the shirt over his head but without success,

45

and finally the girl said, 'Here, let me do that. Bend your head forwards!'

Race did as instructed, and she drew the now bloody garment over his head; then freeing his arms, she threw it on the ground. Taking Race by the right elbow, she steered him to a nearby log and bade him be seated while she examined the knife wound. 'Hmm. That's a nasty cut you have there, though I don't think it's too deep. I may have to sew it up. Is that all right with you, Marshal?

Race tried to twist his head sufficiently to see what she was looking at, but he wasn't that much of a contortionist. 'I guess I'll just have to take your word for it, Miss er...' There was a long pause. '...What exactly is your name? Mine's Munro. Race Munro!'

She offered a long name in her Indian tongue, and then said: 'But at the Mission School where I learned English, the priest called me Rosebud. You may call me that if you wish.'

While she was speaking, she deftly washed away the blood from Race's back; then she called to her mother for assistance, and the two of them sewed up the slit in the flesh over Race's shoulder blade, wisely leaving the lower end open to allow the wound to drain.

While the two women were thus engaged, the old Indian man, having completed his prayers, got to his feet and came over to where Race was sitting, and examined critically their surgical repair work. Apparently satisfied, he expressed his approval with a loud 'Huh' and, placing both horny old hands on

Race's head, chanted a brief benediction in his own tongue.

His actions pleased the two women, and Rosebud was quite impressed that Race had received such a blessing. 'My grandfather, Sitting Bull, is a very famous medicine man, not only among the Hunkpapa Lakota, but among all the Lakota, the people that you white people call the Sioux tribes. It is very unusual that he offers a blessing to one of your tribe.'

Race said very little in reply. He was experiencing a reaction from the rough first aid that had been administered, and he just wanted to sleep – which he did, but it was a disturbed rest, punctuated with dreams of knife- and gunfights, and being ministered to by fair Indian maidens.

While he slept his pony was brought down to the clearing and the pack burden removed, and his saddle taken off the patient sorrel. His bloody shirt was washed and hung up to dry, and the knife rent sewn up.

Then the corpses of the two would-be assassins were wrapped in a couple of old pieces of tarpaulin ready for when Race awoke. The Lakota family had decided what the white marshal should do with the two bodies. It was important that no blame should be laid at their door, as they knew only too well how the white settlers tended to place every wrong at the door of their Indian neighbours. They would not listen to an Indian explanation, and would immediately seek revenge for the murder of two of their tribe.

Race awoke to the smell of something appetizing, and suddenly realized that he had not had anything to eat for a very long time. His left shoulder was throbbing, and was very stiff when he attempted to flex it, prompting a groan from the effort.

Rosebud looked over at the noise and came to squat where he was lying: 'How do you feel now, Marshal? Do you think you could perhaps eat something?'

Race indicated that he was so hungry that he could devour a horse, even with the hair still on it, at which remark Rosebud smiled and left him, only to return with a large bowl of stew and a couple of camp biscuits. Washed down with strong black coffee, the food rapidly disappeared; as the last biscuit crumbs were wiped around the bowl and consumed, Race breathed a deep sigh of contentment and commented: 'That was great, Rosebud. What kind of stew was it?'

She looked at him and smiled. 'Dog stew!' she replied, at which Race regretted asking the question!

The girl helped him put on his mended shirt, and explained the need to remove the two bodies from their little Lakota camp. Race agreed, and indicated that he would take them south to the next white community.

CHAPTER EIGHT

Twelve hours later Race reined in his horse and surveyed the cluster of buildings that a faded sign a mile back had told him was the approach to Gainsville. Back at the Lakota campsite the family had assisted him in lifting the tarpaulin-covered bodies and putting them face down on their horses, lashing them securely into position, then preparing his own animals for travelling. After a series of hearty farewells he had headed south with his strange convoy of pack horse and the two other horses and their cargo.

While riding along Race had had ample time to decide what he would say to explain away the two corpses he was escorting, and hadn't managed to find a satisfactory explanation. He had thought of several stories, including finding the bodies by the side of the trail, but each had a hollow ring when he described it to himself, and he couldn't believe that others would be convinced by his fabrications. Now the time was rapidly approaching when he had to produce some story to explain the two corpses, and still he wasn't sure what to say. But minutes later the issue was resolved for him.

The sorrel, followed by its strange pack train, was plodding along the dusty trail that led between unpainted, weather-warped buildings that represented the business section of Gainsville, while Race looked for a sign indicating 'Marshal' or 'Sheriff', showing that law and order existed in the community. Then a voice called out from the doorway of a structure with the word 'Saloon' prominently displayed.

'Hey, Marshal! Did you get them? Looks like you did, since thems their horses!' and a bald-headed man with a black waxed moustache ran forwards, wiping his hands on the dirty white apron encircling his ample girth. He was followed by others, obviously patrons of his drinking establishment, drawn by the bartender's interest in Race's cargo.

Race had halted, bemused by the bartender's cry, and he sat there making no comment as the latter unwrapped the end of the tarpaulins to peer at the contents. 'Yep! He got them all right! Plumb centre, I'd reckon. Must've bin quite a fight I'd guess?' He looked up in awe at Race Munro as the crowd grew, with others adding more queries, while some demanded that the Marshal be allowed to dispose of his cargo before he answered all their questions.

Race dismounted and raised both hands for silence. 'Folks, you're all talking at once. Let one person do the talking and tell me the whole story from the town's point of view, and then, perhaps, I can fill in the remainder.' Secretly he was relieved that there appeared to be a plausible reason why a stranger would appear in town lugging two bodies.

The bartender, or possibly the owner of the adjacent saloon, appointed himself spokesman. 'My name's Jenks, Marshal,' he said, peering at Race's silver badge, 'Clem Jenks. I'm the owner of the Buffalo Head Saloon, and actually the mayor of our little community. We've never had any real trouble here since the town was founded nigh on ten years ago. Not even with the local Indian population. We treated them fairly, and I must say they have bin good neighbours.

'Well, of late, in the past few months, we've had a different sort of people drifting through. More shiftless, if you know what I mean. Some have bin rowdy, even before taking a drink, and when they've bin into the liquor they've become downright mean. The two you've brought back were like that. Pushy when sober and dirty dog mean when drunk.

'Well, because of the rowdies the town had a meeting an' decided to appoint a sheriff. They spoke to Bill Watson, an' he, a good steady man who fought in the Civil War, agreed to do the job. Actually, for a while it was easy for him. Jus' lock up the odd drunk and do a turn around the town at night and see that all was secure, an' that was that. Then we began to get vandalism from the rowdies. Windows smashed by fellas in their cups an' so forth, and some were getting increasingly belligerent.

'Then Brice Cooper and his sidekick Drew Larson came to town. They had money, but I don't know where they got it from 'cos they never worked. They lodged with Annie Grayson. The widow Grayson that is, and after a short while they started treating her badly, and not showing her the respect that any woman, good or bad, deserves. Eventually, one evening she turned up at the sheriff's office with her poor face all bruised an' puffy, one eye closed from a severe beating, an' her dress half torn from her back.

'Bill went down to the Buffalo Head and confronted the two bullies. At first they tried to pass it all off as just a bit of innocent fun, and when that didn't work, they became very hostile. The sheriff asked for their pistols, and appearing to comply, they drew them – and then they shot him. They stole two horses at the hitching rail and thundered out of town firing at anything that moved.

'That's our story, Marshal. We're a small community, an' although the menfolk would defend their homes, we couldn't raise a posse to go off after those two evil villains, especially since it would leave our families an' the town undefended.'

Race Munro, having heard Gainsville's side of the sorry tale, gave an abbreviated version of what had happened several miles down the trail, of how he had come upon Larson and Cooper terrorizing a single family, and how his objections had led to gun play, with the results under the tarpaulins.

'Well, Marshal Munro, on behalf of the people of Gainsville I thank you for your service, and if there is anything we can do for you, just name it, and we'll do our best to satisfy your requests.'

'Thank you, Mr Jenks, I'm certainly going to take advantage of your kind offer. First of all, could you have someone take these two bodies off my hands. I'm tired of having them follow me around. Second, I'd like someone to look at my shoulder. One of these galoots got a knife into me. It has been sewn up but I'd appreciate if someone would just check out the first aid. Thirdly, I would enjoy a decent meal instead of my own cooking for a change – and finally has anyone seen a tall stranger, with a prominent scar below the left eye down to his chin, passing through town?'

'Marshal, I think that we can most certainly comply immediately with some of your requests.' He motioned to a couple of the bystanders, and they, in response to his signals, took the horses bearing the two bodies away to a building across the street to where the town undertaker operated his business. Another man trotted off to find Doc Parsons, the country physician who attended to the physical needs of the small community. That worthy appeared as Munro was led into the Buffalo Head saloon and was seated at a table while a meal was prepared for him.

Clem Jenks introduced the doctor to the marshal, and the former indicated that the lawman should remove his shirt. Race did so, and Doc Parsons called for a bowl of warm water and gently removed the homemade bandage that was sticking to the knife cut.

'Young fella, I don't know who fixed up this knife cut but they did a good professional job. In a few days if all goes well, get somebody to remove those stitches.' He replaced the bandage with a large piece of sticky plaster that covered the wound, and with the usual advice about taking it easy and keeping that area clean, he departed, refusing the offered fee saying that his work was a service to the community.

While the doctor was checking Race's back, Clem Jenks vanished for a short while, obviously giving instructions in the rear of the building because hardly had Doc Parsons left the saloon when a lady, introduced as Mrs Jenks, came forth from the kitchen bearing a huge plate upon which was a very large fried steak floating in a sea of beans and topped by three fried eggs. Balanced precariously on the edge of the plate were two thick slices of home-made bread, which the marshal was told had been baked that very morning.

Mrs Jenks placed the meal on the table where Race was sitting, then vanished and returned with a big mug of steaming black coffee and a thick wedge of apple pie. 'For your dessert when you've finished your steak,' the good lady said.

Race fell to and rapidly demolished the steak and its accompanying food, but didn't feel sated until he'd wiped the plate clean with the last piece of bread; then after eyeing the pie, ate every morsel of it, washing it down with swigs of coffee.

Race was silent while he broke his long fast, and having finished his meal, stretched out his long legs and, placing both hands on his stomach, uttered a very satisfied 'Ah! That was fantastic. Thank you!'

Clem Jenks was delighted that the marshal had enjoyed his meal, but now that it was finished he was eager to impart the information that Race had been seeking. 'Marshal, that fella you've bin huntin' – the scarred man. Was he riding a horse with a white blaze? If that's your man he passed through here about a week ago. Left a played-out bronc in the corral. I understand he traded it with Silas at the livery stable for a sack of grain. Could be that's your man!'

Race rose wearily from the seat where he had just finished his meal, 'Well, I guess we'd better take a look at this animal and see if it might be the one.' He followed Clem Jenks out of the saloon and diagonally across the street to the livery stable, and then through the stable barn to the corral at the rear. There at the near side of the enclosure was a brownish grey mare, and when she raised her head slowly to see the two humans watching her, the white blaze was very apparent.

'Polly! Come here Polly!' And the mare came along to stand with her head over the corral bars waiting for her nose to be scratched.

Race turned to Clem Jenks. 'That mare belonged to a young man named Kurt Vogel. He was murdered by the same villain I've been pursuing.'

CHAPTER NINE

Bill Westerman's plans had not worked out as he had intended. He had originally joined the NWMP with the thought of cutting a fine appearance, strutting around in uniform to the envy of other men and the admiration of all the ladies. The march west had been a bitter disappointment to him, and soon after the march had commenced, he had begun to hate every hour that he stayed with the force. He was not alone in the disillusionment felt by a number of the would-be heroes of the West.

A number had in fact deserted, and there were times when he wished that he had gone with them. Westerman, however, lacked the type of courage to just take off, especially since the possibilities of being captured were very real. And so he kept his thoughts to himself. To his fellow troopers and the NCOs of the Force, he presented the image of a reliable but taciturn man.

When Corporal Munro approached Trooper Vogel and himself with the chance of going south of the border into American territory, and in civilian cloth-ing, Westerman realized that his big chance had come, especially when he thought they would be carrying a large sum of money on the journey to Fort Benson.

From that moment on it was merely a question of choosing the right moment. For a while he consid-ered the idea of getting young Vogel to join him in any plan, but rejected the notion on two points. One, he thought that the man was just too honest to join in such a venture, and two, more importantly, he, Bill Westerman, would have to share whatever money he acquired. After due consideration he decided to oper-ate as a lone hand. From the time the trio crossed the border he was constantly watching for the moment when he could put his plan into operation.

On the second day, as they passed a delightful glade among the trees alongside the trail, his oppor-tunity arose. Corporal Munro, reckoning that a short halt and maybe a quick coffee would be welcome, had suggested that they have such a rest.

While the corporal wrote up his report and young Vogel busied himself at the fire, Westerman had taken his Snider carbine from its scabbard and indicated that he was just going to look around, as he thought that he'd seen someone beneath the trees. After that everything went according to plan.

He walked over to the trees carrying his carbine at the high port with the weapon at half cock and with his right thumb beneath the breech catch. Reaching the trees, he flipped open the breech block, dropped in one of the heavy .577 cartridges, pushed it home in the chamber and closing the breech, brought the hammer to full cock as he turned, brought the piece to his shoulder and fired. His target was the back of Corporal Munro's head, and with the explosion, his first victim fell forwards from his seated position.

With not a moment to lose, Westerman flipped the Snider breech open to the right and pulled it back to extract the smoking fired cartridge. A quick twist of the wrist dropped the empty shell into the grass, and the weapon was swiftly reloaded.

While these actions were taking place Kurt Vogel had stared horrified, first at his fellow trooper, then at the corporal's bloody head, and then back at Westerman – he then turned to run, but that initial hesitation cost him his life as the assassin coolly raised the carbine and shot him in the back, smashing his spine and causing his instant death.

Westerman had reloaded, but there was no need as both of his victims were undoubtedly dead. There was no movement from either man, but to be sure he walked forwards and poked with the muzzle of the gun first Vogel's recumbent face-down form, then that of the corporal. There was still no indication of life in either of them, and leaving them where they lay, he walked, satisfied, over to where the packs lay.

He rummaged through Corporal Munro's saddle-bags, tossing out the spare shirt, socks and underwear – but there was absolutely nothing that resembled money in any form. There was a cleaning kit for Munro's rifle and pistol, several letters tied with a piece of string, a towel and soap along with a razor, and two novels, one by Sir Walter Scott and the other by Charles Dickens – but no money.

In frustration Westerman turned to Kurt Vogel's kit and gave it the same treatment, but the contents of the trooper's saddlebags proved to be even more meagre than those of the corporal. Spare clothing, cleaning materials for both the man and his weapons, and a well thumbed English/ German dictionary were the only things that he discovered – no money.

Wildly Westerman stared around. It appeared that he had killed his two comrades for nothing, and anyone passing by would immediately associate him with the two corpses lying by the now smouldering campfire. He had to get as far away as possible to avoid being accused of murder. Was there anything he could gain from the crime he had committed? Well, he could take the other firearms – the carbines and the two revolvers should fetch something. Also the other two horses could be sold or traded at some future point in time. Was there anything else?

His eyes flickered from the saddlebags to the now dead owners, and rested on the elegant boots worn by the corporal. Westerman had always admired those boots, and since their owner no longer needed them, he decided he might as well take them. He did so, throwing his own old cracked ones into the undergrowth; then gathering his spoils and quickly saddling his own horse, he mounted up and with one last hurried look round, left the clearing of death leading the other animals.

As he rode along, still following the trail leading to Fort Benson, Westerman tried to consider his position objectively. In all his planning, during the march west, he hadn't really thought what he would do once he possessed the money he thought would be his. Oh, sure, he intended to have a good time. With money jingling in his pockets he'd have no trouble picking up a woman whenever he wanted one, and he wouldn't have to rely purely on soiled doves. With money he could buy a more classy kind of female. Westerman, never having had money, thought that with it he would be able to buy anything he wanted.

Now the situation had completely changed. By killing Munro and Vogel he had put himself beyond the pale, and he knew he must get away from the border area as swiftly as possible. In a short while Colonel French would be coming down the trail to Fort Benson with men and wagons, and woe betide him if he fell into their hands.

With all these thoughts swimming around in his head, Bill Westerman urged his steed and the two he was leading to quicken their gait in order to reach Fort Benson sooner. He made a dry camp that evening, picketing the three horses, and had a restless night starting at every noise – whenever he wearily closed his eyes he was immediately confronted by the image of one of his victims staring at him and pointing with bloodstained hands. He would waken with a jolt and peer around, terrified at what he might encounter. There was nothing out there, of course, and he would sink back relieved and finally close his eyes – only for the whole scenario to start again. And so Bill Westerman passed his first night as a murderer.

Two days later he was approaching Fort Benson, but he avoided the military establishment, confining his attentions to the medley of shacks, soddies and frame buildings that were the civilian portion of the community. Apart from a few coppers in his pocket he was penniless, and his first objective was to get some money. Seeing the giant symbol of a rifle above the sign 'Gunsmith', it occurred to him that perhaps he could sell the two Snider carbines carried on one of the spare horses.

He tied the three horses to the hitching rail, and mounting the steps to the boardwalk, took a deep breath, pushed open the door and hurried inside.

'Mr Schultz?' Westerman enquired of the bald-headed smiling man behind the counter, diligently polishing his spectacles.

'Ja, you know me?'

Bill Westerman hurriedly gave a negative reply to that query, but explained that he had seen the name on the signboard. 'I have a couple of guns I'm thinking of selling. Won them in a card game up near the Canadian border. I was wondering what you'd give me for them? May I bring them in?'

John Schultz nodded his assent, and Westerman hurried out, then returned with the two guns, which he placed on the counter. The gunsmith stood looking at them silently for a full two minutes, pursing his lips and making 'Tch Tch' sounds. Then he picked up first one and then the other, opening and closing the breech of each and peering down the muzzle with his thumbnail in the open chamber.

'Dese are jus single shot guns. Everybody's lookin' for magazine long guns today. I don' think that I…'

But Bill Westerman interrupted him: 'I just want to get rid of them. You can have them both for a good fair price. You're bound to make a profit when you sell 'em!' he concluded hopefully.

John Schultz looked at the two carbines and then at the pleading face before him, and relented, saying 'OK, I vill give you five dollars for each' – and then obliging him a little more, said 'No, I vill give you eleven dollars for de two.'

Westerman shrugged his shoulders, 'OK, Mr Schultz. If that's your last word on the subject, I guess I'll just have to take the eleven dollars.'

The gunsmith carefully counted out eleven silver dollars on to the counter, and Westerman pocketed them; as he left the shop John Schultz placed the two Snider carbines up in his long gun rack. With money in his pocket Westerman did what he had wanted to do now for several days: he crossed Main Street, entered a neighbouring saloon and quickly downed a beer, and then a second one while he considered his next plan of action.

His third beer he drank slowly, almost sipping it, while he listened to the talk going on around him. Men talked excitedly about supposed gold strikes being made elsewhere in the West, and of fortunes being amassed by the discoveries of other precious metals. Others declared that California on the Pacific coast was the place to head for, as gold could be picked up by the handful there – and if one had the desire to grow things, the trees and vines were so bountiful that settlers could pick two or three harvests of fruit each year.

But for Bill Westerman there was a very dark side to all the fanciful dreams of wealth that he heard. First you had to get to these far-off places, and each route was beset with more problems than many wished to contend with. Blizzards blocked the routes in winter, and there were deserts to cross, long, dry stretches where the unprepared ended up as desiccated bundles of bones – and above all there was the constant threat of hostile Indians.

He heard stories of individuals, of small parties of civilians as well as soldiers, and even of wagon trains being attacked, and in many cases massacred to the last soul. It appeared that the Sioux nation and their cousins the northern Cheyenne were particularly restless.

Westerman considered going east into the Black Hills, where he understood that gold was plentiful.

However, realistically he knew this was impossible, as he had neither the tools for mining nor the food supplies, nor did he know anybody who would grubstake him. Eventually, as he finished his beer, Bill Westerman decided that he would head south towards Fort Ellis and see if he could link up with folks heading west on the Bozeman Trail towards the Pacific coast.

In a general store in Fort Benson he bought a few extra supplies to augment those he had taken when he had left the clearing and the two NWMP corpses. Using his money in miserly fashion he spent three dollars on a small side of bacon, dried beans, coffee, dried apples and a bag of locally made corn dodgers.

Thus equipped, Westerman headed south. He kept strictly to himself, and ignored or merely responded with a curt nod the greetings from fellow travellers. A bunch of young men lolling at the side of the trail drinking and shouting to each other with raucous glee invited him to join in their merriment, but he hurried on, intent on putting as many miles as possible between himself and the arrival at Fort Benson of Colonel French, who would be his Nemesis.

Then trooper Vogel's horse started limping, and after determining that it did not have a stone in its hoof, he ascertained the problem was in its hock, which, upon closer examination, was quite swollen. Westerman hated the notion of just turning the horse loose, since it represented money to him, and in Gainsville he managed to trade in the horse for a sack of grain, which was appreciated by the remaining two animals.

He remained in Gainsville for two days, during which time he camped in a small copse of trees on the edge of town. He never went into the saloon, The Buffalo Head, and apart from the livery stable owner, had no discourse with a single soul.

When he figured that the horses were sufficiently rested, he left the Gainsville area, still with the western trail as his ultimate objective. Maybe it was a guilty conscience that prompted him to periodically look behind him down the trail. 'Don't be ridiculous, Bill,' he told himself. 'There is no reason why anybody should suspect you to be anything other than an innocent traveller. Munro and Vogel are both dead and have probably long since provided food for the buzzards and other scavengers. As far as Colonel French is concerned, well, he'll arrive at Fort Benson to find the advance patrol never even got there, and he may well think that all three deserted, like so many other erstwhile members of the NWMP.'

CHAPTER TEN

Thus comforted in his thoughts, Westerman rode south, still on the lookout for the opportunity of increasing his slender supply of ready cash. Three days later the chance presented itself. Noticing a cabin nestled against a bluff on the eastern side of the trail, half hidden by a screen of aspens and other foliage, he decided to try and replenish his canteen, since a habitation indicated a source of water. Riding through the trees he openly approached the cabin, and halted immediately a figure appeared in the doorway of the well constructed shack.

'Hello the house! Could you spare some water for me and my critturs, if it's not too much trouble?'

'No trouble at all, stranger! You'll have to draw it from the well. We keep intending to install a pump, but have never got around to it. Still, it's good clean water an' we've thrived on it. Ain't we Martha?' This last statement was said over his shoulder to a grey-haired, elderly woman who was peering through the cabin's one window.

'Name's Lucas, Ephraim Lucas. God knows why my parents stuck me with a name like that, but they did. Most folks call me Eph. And who might I be addressing?'

Although as a general rule in the West one did not inquire too deeply into a stranger's name or place of origin, Westerman could hardly take offence at Eph's courteous query, and he was compelled to respond: 'Smith, Bill Smith, Mr Lucas!' Westerman answered curtly. Then he went to the well and drew up a bucketful, which he poured into the nearby trough. He continued the operation of filling the trough, then led both horses forwards so they could drink their fill; all the while the garrulous old-timer kept up a steady patter of information about himself and Martha his wife, interwoven with oblique questions, to which Bill Westerman tried to give vague replies.

Then Eph Lucas vanished into the cabin, to reappear almost immediately just as Bill finished filling his canteen, with the query: 'Say Bill, are you in a hurry? How would you like a nice home-cooked meal? Martha's just fixing up lunch for us, and you're mighty welcome to join us!'

Bill Westerman thought for a brief moment, then realizing that such a stay would not hinder his plans, he readily assented to the invitation. His hostess was a thin, elderly lady with careworn features, but nevertheless sprightly in her movements; she was also a very good plain cook, and the three of them sat down to a large bowl of thick stew with small Irish potatoes, green beans grown behind the cabin, and also a pile of hot biscuits, followed by raisin pie washed down with copious quantities of thick black coffee.

Afterwards while Martha cleared away the dirty dishes, the two men sat yarning over yet more mugs of coffee.

'Say, Bill! Were you ever in the cavalry?'

'Er, no Eph! Why would you ask such a question?' queried Westerman, agitated that Lucas might have spotted something that revealed some aspect of his past.

'Well now, don't get het up about it, fella. It's just that you talk like an Easterner, not like the folks hereabouts – but what is more to the point, you carry your pistol in a military holster with the flap buttoned down. Now, don't get me wrong, I've nothing against the military. Served in an Ohio regiment myself during the Civil War. Here, let me show you.'

Eph rose from the table and crossed the room to a shelf, from which he took down a tin box; he placed it on the table and then carefully opened it. Amid a medley of papers, receipts, family photographs and other items, was a regimental cap badge and a medal for good conduct, which he laid on the table proudly.

Bill Westerman feigned interest in his host's war mementos, but actually his interest was drawn to the glint of gold in the box. This old fool was showing that they had money stashed away, and didn't even realize it. Slowly, while looking at the two objects on the table, he unfastened his holster flap under the cover of a green tablecloth, and as Eph started to replace the articles in the box, Bill produced his Adams revolver and made his move: 'Just a minute old man! I'll relieve you of that box! Leave it where it is and step away, an' you won't get hurt!'

Ephraim Lucas literally quivered with rage. 'You filthy ingrate! We give you our hospitality and this is how you would repay us!' He darted to where a Springfield trapdoor rifle stood loaded in the corner of the cabin.

As his hand seized the barrel Westerman fired, the bullet striking the old man in the back under the left shoulder blade. Eph collapsed, and as he made an effort to rise, he received a second killing shot that left him huddled on the floor in the corner.

As Westerman had fired his second shot he was pounded on the back of the head by an enraged Martha, wielding a heavy cast-iron skillet. 'Murderer!' she screamed as she raised the utensil in order to deliver yet another blow, repeatedly screaming 'Murderer! Murderer!' Bill, partially stunned, turned and fired one shot that smashed into the woman's sternum, driving her back until she fell to the floor against the kitchen sink.

Bill Westerman, revolver in hand, sat motionless for a while, shocked by the enormity of the crime that he had perpetrated; then seizing the box that had prompted him to act as he had done, he tipped its contents on the table. Feverishly he pushed aside the collection of documents, faded letters, bills and photographs to seize upon the glittering remainder of the contents. He was aghast at what he discovered.

There in front of him were a half-dozen brass curtain rings, enough polished brass buttons to fit two full dress Union uniforms, a brass whistle, nine assorted brass cartridge cases, and a single twenty-dollar gold piece! That was all. He had wantonly killed two innocent people for a small pile of trash!

The enormity of his crime, far worse even than the murder of his two comrades, shook him to his very core and he knew that he was forever damned – unless? His twisted mind tried to reason with his conscience. If he could get away, maybe he could make good somehow – do some great deed somewhere, which would cancel out the terrible things that he had done.

Westerman stumbled from the cabin, reloading and holstering his Adams as he did so. He looked around wildly with the thought that someone might have seen him, and running over to where the two horses were tethered, he unhitched them and mounting one, hurried from the location back to the main trail.

He had been heading south-west, intending to pass through Great Falls on his way to where he thought he could pick up the Bozeman Trail, but now all was changed, and he decided to go east, away from the route that he had planned. Not far south from where he had watered the horses he saw a weathered board with the words 'Barton's Creek' crudely painted on it, half hidden by the bushes, pointing to a gravelled track leading up into the hills. Westerman decided to take it. Being a stony surface it would be more difficult for anyone to track his passage, and by the way the trail was overgrown it was obvious that it was some while since anyone had passed this way.

As he travelled further away from the main trail he found himself engaged in a mental battle, with one side saying that he was forever doomed because of his actions, while the other half justified his actions.

'There was no need to wantonly kill those two elderly people.'

'But he was trying to get a gun! He would have killed me, so I had to kill him.'

'Well, what about old Martha? There was no excuse for that!'

'Oh yes there was, she attacked me when I hadn't done anything to her. She would have beaten my brains out. I was only defending myself!'

And even the horses' hooves appeared to join in the dispute as they trotted along, saying 'Murderer! Murderer!' until Westerman finally halted, thinking that with the hooves silenced he might gain a little peace.

It was not to be. While the two horses rested his mind flitted back to a scene when he had been a few years younger. Being between casual jobs he had deliberately gone to Goderich, Ontario, for one specific purpose: he and hundreds of others, men women and a fair sprinkling of children, went to watch a public hanging.

Nicholas Melady was to be hung for the murder of his father and his stepmother. The hanging was set for 7 December 1869, and since the trial had attracted a great deal of attention across southern Ontario, a large number of viewers were expected to attend, especially since rumour had it that this would be the last public hanging in Ontario.

Westerman recalled that the execution had been a very curious affair. The gallows had been built on the wall of Huron County gaol. The condemned man would walk unseen up the steps to the gallows plat-form, where he could be seen by the crowd. When the trap was sprung he would fall below on the out-side of the prison wall.

Despite all the scientific preparations, things did not go as had been planned. Melady's neck did not snap with the drop, and the onlookers watched as the condemned man fought desperately for life, drawing up his legs so his knees were level with his chest, while his body writhed frantically from side to side in a vain effort to obtain air. But gradually his move-ments had become slower, and finally, minutes later, they ceased, while simultaneously the crowd let out an 'ah' of expelled air.

Westerman, like many of the assembled men, had instinctively put his hand to his neck and loosened his woollen 'choker' scarf, with the vow that he, William

Westerman, would live his life in such a way that he would never experience the hangman's noose. And now fate had created a situation where he had to flee for his life or, quite possibly, face the same destiny as Nicholas Melady.

After this short halt Westerman urged his horses on, determined to put all the past, whether recent events or distant history, out of his mind and to concentrate solely on what was most important: his own survival.

CHAPTER ELEVEN

Race Munro left Gainsville refreshed, and with the good wishes of the townsfolk ringing in his ears, along with cries of 'Don't forget to come back and see us, Marshal!' But despite making enquiries of every person he encountered on the trail thereafter, he discovered nothing that indicated he was close to his quarry.

Then, three days south of Gainsville, he saw a knot of people in animated conversation gathered by the side of the trail. One raised his hand as Race drew near. 'Hold it right there stranger! Where are you from, and where are you headed?' Then suddenly his eyes opened wide as he noticed the small silver badge on Race's jacket.

'Gee, I'm sorry, Marshal. It's just that we're stopping everyone passing by, seeking to find out if anyone can give us a clue as to what happened here.'

'Well mister, maybe it would help if you could explain what exactly did happen here?' declared Race a trifle tartly at the man's attitude. 'Then you might have a perfectly good reason for stopping people!'

'If you could just leave your horses here Marshal, and walk with me up to that cabin, you'll see why we're all het up.' Race did as suggested, and on the way, the local man introduced himself as Robert – commonly known as Bob – Spengler, a neighbour of Ephraim Lucas who had lived in the cabin they were approaching. Bob had been coming with a dozen eggs as a gift when he encountered a small group of other neighbours already at the site, wondering who could have killed the old couple.

Arriving at the lonely cabin Bob introduced Marshal Munro to the other people present and they respectfully stepped to one side so that he could enter and examine the scene of the crime. After ascertaining that nothing had been moved since the initial discovery, he stood silently examining the interior of the cabin.

An old man lay huddled in a far corner surrounded by a pool of blood now soaking into the pine boards of the floor. A rifle for which he had obviously been reaching lay on top of his body. The body of an elderly woman, probably his wife, was crumpled up on the floor in front of a dry sink and a number of recently washed dishes. The old lady was still grasping an iron skillet in her right hand.

On the rough-hewn table a small number of curtain rings, buttons and cartridge cases were spread out next to a collection of paper and faded photographs.

It seemed obvious that robbery had been the motive, and that the robber had reacted violently when interrupted in his thievery. There was nothing Race could do in this case, and he decided to advise the local people to contact their county sheriff.

As he was turning towards the door with the intention of imparting that advice, one of the other men present thrust out a clenched hand, exclaiming 'Say, Marshal! I don't know whether this is important, but I found these shell cases just outside the door of the cabin.'

He solemnly handed Race three empty cartridge cases, which the pseudo marshal took, amazed at the stupidity of people who would conceal what could be valuable evidence at a crime scene.

'Where did you find these?' queried Race while he examined the three stubby brass cases and drew one of his Colt shells from the loops in his gun-belt for comparison.

It was as he had suspected. The Colt case was about one and a quarter inches in length, whereas the ones handed to him, though of approximately the same diameter and therefore about the same calibre, were much shorter, being just under three-quarters of an inch in length. For final confirmation, Race examined the base of the short case. There was no head stamp indicating either calibre or manufacturer, and to his knowledge there was only one type of shell that fitted that bill, and that was the Adams cartridge.

His blood ran cold as he half listened to the fellow's admission that he had found the cases just outside the cabin door and had intended to keep them as a curiosity, but had then thought that maybe they might be important, so had decided to hand them over.

'I hope you realize that by withholding evidence you would be committing a crime!' Race paused while he invented a possible sentence for such an offence. 'And you could be ordered to serve a sentence of not less than six months!' with which he dismissed the offender with a wave of his hand, as he realized the full implications of the three empty shell cases.

He walked away from the group by the doorway and appeared to be studying the ground while he pondered the situation. It was obvious from the cartridge cases that Bill Westerman had committed the two murders. But why? And the answer followed the question. The deserter was short of money. He had obviously thought that when he had killed his corporal and trooper Vogel he would obtain money, in which he had not been successful. Then he had sold two of the stolen Snider carbines to obtain funds, and later traded a horse for a sack of grain. Now he had turned his hand to still more killing to obtain money.

Race knew that he just had to catch this evil-hearted villain, because he strongly suspected that, getting more desperate, Westerman would find it easier to kill, time and time again, as he attempted to satisfy his desires. Fortunately, of one thing Race was sure: Westerman did not yet know that he was being pursued.

Race turned back to the small group, its members waiting expectantly for him to make a pronouncement on the case. He addressed Bob Spengler, who appeared to be the self-appointed spokesman of the local population.

'Bob! There is nothing more that I can do here. I'm sure that between you all you can arrange the funeral and religious observances for these unfortunate people. Regarding their murderer, I know who committed this crime. He's a deliberate killer who shot a young man north of Fort Benson about three weeks ago, and I've been on his trail ever since. Sadly I didn't catch up with him before this tragedy occurred.'

Grim-faced, Race nodded goodbye to the assembled men, and striding down to the main trail, suggested to the people waiting there that they check with Bob Spengler for information as he had to make haste after his quarry. With this parting remark he mounted his sorrel, and spurring it into a canter, headed south, with the little grey mare following behind.

Rounding a curve that hid him from the folk discussing the murder of the people at the Lucas cabin, he slowed down and finally halted. He desperately needed time to think, and found it difficult to concentrate while dealing with the problems of a local crime.

Where would Bill Westerman have gone, having killed yet again? Race rode on slowly, informing everyone he encountered that he was seeking a tall, face-scarred man riding one horse and leading another, and asking if they had seen him. Most people tried to be helpful, especially when they saw his marshal's badge, but all responses were negative, and eventually Race began to think that possibly he might be following the wrong trail.

Eventually about fifteen miles south of the Lucas cabin he was offered a suggestion that he decided could possibly be the answer to his problem. He had stopped to speak to a middle-aged couple busy building a large cabin by the side of the trail, a cabin they enthusiastically told him would one day become a wayside hotel catering to the trade between Fort Benson and Great Falls.

When Race finally succeeded in stemming their eagerness to share their dreams long enough to pose his question, the female of the couple said in an off-hand fashion, 'Marshal, do you think perhaps your man could have gone off on one of the side trails leading up into the hills?'

Race was bewildered. 'What side trails? I didn't see any side trails between the Lucas cabin and this spot.'

'Oh, there is one, to Barton's Creek. It's probably overgrown a bit by now as not many would go that way, but it's there all right. You'll find it on the eastern side, about a mile south of the Lucas place. You'll have to look carefully, as you can easily miss the turn-off. There used to be a sign, but maybe it's gone now. If you reach the small stream that crosses the main trail you have gone too far north.'

Race, having thanked them for their assistance, turned his animals about and headed north, inwardly cursing his own lack of observation. He set the pace at a sharp canter, and in time, seeing the ford some distance ahead where the stream crossed the trail, he slowed his horse's pace to a walk as he sought any sign a of side trail on his right side.

Ah! There it was – an overgrown pathway winding up between the trees, and almost hidden in the undergrowth was the faded sign pointing the way to Barton's Creek. Race followed the dim trail onwards and up among the rounded hills, noting from the crushed grass and the occasional broken twigs that a horse or horses had passed that way recently. Further evidence was provided by a healthy pile of horse droppings, not more than a couple of days old.

CHAPTER TWELVE

The hours passed, and still the dim winding trail led on between the heavily wooded hills. Then gradually, the scene ahead began to change. The trees were spaced further apart, and increasingly consisted of secondary growth, with stumps showing in the under-growth where the original giants had once stood. A cabin appeared, or rather the remains of somebody's long vanished ambitions, with the roof fallen in and gaping holes that were once door and windows.

As he proceeded he passed other abandoned dwellings, indicating that this isolated location may once have been a thriving community. The stream that he had encountered down on the main trail now reappeared, and widened into a shallow pool close on twenty feet across; along one side were several wooden buildings, dominated by one that possessed a large faded sign above its covered porch, stating that here was Barton's Creek General Store and Saloon.

There were no animals at the hitching rail, and no lights were showing in the gathering gloom since the afternoon was far advanced, so the place gave the impression that it was absolutely deserted.

Race drew closer, and as he did so, first one light and then another came on in the store or saloon. He halted at the hitching rail and dismounted, looping the sorrel's reins in a 'get-away' knot; then climbing up to the boardwalk, he crossed to the double doors. He paused momentarily, glancing around, and then, slipping his Colt up and down a couple of times to ensure it was not jammed in its holster, he pushed on the left-hand door and stepped inside and to the right, where he halted and surveyed the interior scene.

Facing him was a long bar, which extended three-quarters of the way across the width of the building. Most of the rear wall was dominated by a large rectangular mirror, in front of which was a shelf containing stacks of glasses and the saloon's stock of alcoholic beverages in various bottles of assorted shapes and sizes. Behind the bar stood a portly man in a clean white apron wearing a blue-and-white long-sleeved shirt and sporting a heavily waxed moustache.

The patrons of this establishment were few and silent, apart from one customer seated at a table by himself who was demanding yet another bottle of rye whiskey to replace the empty one lying on the floor at his feet. The man – dark-haired, bearded, and wearing dark range clothing – turned his head in the direction of the bar as he repeated his demand: 'Damn your hide, Barton! I said bring me another bottle of that rotgut you call whiskey, and I mean now, not next week!'

The barman, and evidently owner of the saloon, had noted Munro's entrance and his eyes had widened at the sight of the small badge prominently displayed on the stranger's coat. Now, therefore, instead of responding to the bearded character's insistent demand for more alcohol, he called out in a pleasant voice: 'Good evening, Marshal! Is there anything we can do for you, or is this a social visit? Either way you're heartily welcome!'

Nobody knows for sure what Joe Barton's intention really was when he greeted Marshal Munro, but it precipitated a violent clash between the lawman and the bearded bully. At the word 'marshal' the latter had sat upright as though he had received an electric shock, and had then sprung to his feet in a gunman's crouch, his right hand hovering just above a tied-down Remington.

'God rot you, lawdog! I thought I'd seen the last of your lot when we did for your partner in Great Falls, but you're like a plague an' keep turnin' up! You might have done for my brother Billy, but you ain't takin' Jake Garner to no hoosegow!'

With the last remark Garner made a savage grab at his low-slung revolver, and Race responded like-wise. Although he was still in the process of becoming familiar with his recently purchased Colt, he had always been considered a natural shot with a pistol, and in the NWMP had won a number of impromptu competitions.

Therefore he drew and fired from the hip in one fluid movement. Jake Garner had his weapon cocked and at forty-five degrees when the 250-grain bullet, propelled by 40 grains of black powder, slammed into him two inches above his belt buckle. The result was devastating in the close quarters of the saloon. Jake was driven back and ended up seated against the wall, with both hands pressed to his gut from which emerged a steady flow of blood.

His pistol had dropped from his hand, and Race kicked it away as he stepped forwards, staring down at the dying man. He was joined by Joe Barton, who looked at Jake Garner and then at Race, shaking his head: 'Marshal, that man has been terrorizing our little community for the best part of a week, and there was little we could do about it. He boasted of having shot and killed a marshal south of Great Falls. He claimed it was revenge because his brother had died while robbing a bank. Somehow, in his twisted mind, he blamed all law officers for his brother's death, and boasted that the one he'd killed recently was just the first. I think it's a good job that you came along when you did.'

Race interrupted him. 'Did you have another visitor riding through recently? A tall man with a prominent scar down the side of his face?'

'Why yes, Marshal, we did. He left a played-out horse here. I gave him ten dollars for the animal and he went on. Do you have paper on him too, Marshal?'

'Actually, I didn't have a warrant for Jake Garner, Mr Barton. He chose to think I had, and acted accordingly. It's strange, because if he hadn't reacted he could have sat there all evening. As it is he caused his own death. The scar-faced fellow I mentioned is wanted for at least three murders in Montana, and I'm anxious to meet up with him before he kills again. If you've got a place where I can get my head down I'll stay the one night and leave in the morning.'

'Marshal, I've got a nice place you can have behind the saloon, and I'll even fix some breakfast. Do you want your two animals out front put in the livery stable? There'll be no extra charge.'

Barton motioned to two of the silent customers, and rising, they carried the body of the dead outlaw out and to a nearby shed to await burial; then one of them attended to Race's two horses, waiting patiently at the hitching rail. Meanwhile, Munro crossed to the bar and gratefully accepted the drink that the saloon keeper poured for him.

Race was feeling deadly tired and would quite willingly have hit the sack, but he felt obliged to listen to Joe Barton's account of the rise and fall of Barton's Creek.

'Marshal, I guess our little community must have appeared a sorry-looking place when you first caught sight of it. Well, you should know it wasn't always like this. Four years ago it was considered a boom town.

Gold had been discovered and people flocked to the Creek – and even when the discovery turned out to be literally just the proverbial 'flash in the pan', they stayed, since there were rumours that a railroad spur line was heading this way, which would have opened up the whole area.

'But the railroad talk turned out to be just that, talk, and folks started to leave for other opportunities. The population has steadily dwindled so now there's no more than a couple of dozen people in the whole...' Joe Barton broke off his description as the door opened to admit another potential customer.

'Well, howdy Mr Weston! Fancy seeing you again!' As he greeted the new arrival, he turned towards Race and flickered his eyes to warn the marshal that this was the scarred man he sought.

Race Munro turned to look at who his host was addressing, and saw a tall man with his collar turned up and his wide-brimmed hat pulled down low over his eyes. Then the man pushed his sombrero further back on his head – and froze as he stared at the marshal in stupefaction.

'Race Munro!' he ejaculated, staring across the saloon at the bar and at the man he had thought was long since dead. 'It can't be you! I killed you!' and he brushed one hand across his eyes as though to wipe away the figure that he saw before him. And then, as the full realization came to him of what would happen in the next moment if he didn't make the first move, he reached behind him, grabbed the door handle and, wrenching the door open, leapt through the doorway. He bounded to the rail, and throwing himself into the saddle, galloped frantically up the trail from Barton's Creek.

CHAPTER THIRTEEN

How could Munro still be alive, and how had he trailed him? In his mind's eye he distinctly saw the corporal face down in the dirt with blood pouring from the hole in his head. There was no way that anyone could have survived that head shot, was there? Surely he had made a mistake, and the man at the bar couldn't possibly have been Corporal Race Munro.

But no, Munro had distinctly recognized him, and thinking back, he seemed to recall the man silently framing the word 'Bill' a split second before he himself dashed for the doorway. And there was certainly no mistake about the shot fired in his general direction as his horse thundered away from Barton's Creek.

What on earth had prompted him to double back on his tracks and risk capture, just to spend an affable evening for once with fellow mankind, instead of being continually on the dodge? Nobody had given him away. Joe Barton had greeted him cheerily, using the name he had adopted the first time that he had gone there. Now as Bill Weston he would be hunted across Montana – unless… He slowed his horse and, as he did so, his racing thoughts also slowed, as he considered his problem with Munro on his trail.

He would have to get rid of Munro. The corporal had to be hunting for him. There was absolutely no reason why Munro should have turned up at Barton's Creek unless somehow he had traced his, Westerman's, route from north of Fort Benson. Yes, he would have to choose a suitable spot and make sure of the job this time, and no mistake about it.

And the deserter rode on through the night heartened by his proposed plan of action, merely waiting for first light when he could start to look for a suitable killing ground.

CHAPTER
FOURTEEN

Race had been attempting to put the sight of the dying Jake Garner out of his mind, and was listening carefully to all that Joe Barton was telling him about the varied fortunes of the Creek when the latter had paused and called out to the individual who had just entered the saloon.

The marshal had looked up as, at the very same moment, the newcomer had pushed his hat back on his head revealing his shadowed features. The livid scar down the side of his face was quite apparent, despite a beard growth of several days adorning his chin. But it wasn't just the scar: Race saw in the new arrival the man who had paraded with him every day for several months. They had been companions along with others in the same bell tent in the nights of the great march west, and had laughed at the same jokes and at the same pranks which relieved the discipline from time to time.

But at the same time as he looked at Bill Westerman he also saw Trooper Kurt Vogel lying with a .577 bullet hole in his back. 'Westerman!' he cried, 'I want you!'

As Race moved forwards, Westerman turned in a flash and was gone. Race rushed after the fleeing man just in time to see him head up the trail at a full gallop in the gathering gloom. Race had drawn his Colt as he ran forwards, and he fired one wild shot after the fugitive; then holstering his pistol he walked back into the saloon.

In response to Joe Barton's enquiring look he shrugged his shoulders and admitted that: 'He got away! It's too dark to pursue him tonight – I'll take up the chase in the morning. Now, Joe, if you can provide me with that bed, I'm gonna turn in.'

The following morning, after a full breakfast of sausage and flapjacks with homemade maple syrup washed down with strong black coffee, Race prepared to depart. Joe Barton refused to accept the proffered money that the marshal wanted to give him for the night's rest: 'No, Marshal, that's all right! You don't owe me a red cent. You did me an' the whole community a great service, getting rid of Jake Garner, so let's say we're quits. Now I hope that you're just as successful with this Westerman character.

'You take care of yourself now, and watch both the trail and the weather. I suspect we're just seeing the end of this Indian summer, and the change can be quite sudden in these parts.'

Race thanked the saloon keeper for his services, and stuffing into a saddlebag the packet of food Joe Barton gave to him to eat on the trail, he shook hands with him, and with the lad who brought his horses from the stable. Then swinging into the saddle, he departed from Barton's Creek.

There was a bite in the wind coming down from the north as Race headed along the trail that led still further up into the hills, and he hoped that Joe Barton had been wrong in his weather forecast. The wind was strong, gusting periodically and raising flurries of dust that prompted the rider to squint, as both he and his two animals faced into the icy gale.

Race found it difficult to maintain a keen lookout for any sign of Westerman as he struggled against the elements and the increasingly difficult nature of the trail. This was no longer bounded by forest on either side, but was now leading across the side of a steep range of hills, with stunted trees to his right and a very steep tree- and bush-covered slope falling away on his left side. To make matters worse the occasional snowflake was landing on his face, and these were increasing with every second, heralding a potential blizzard.

Suddenly the sorrel stumbled, and almost simultaneously Race heard the report of a heavy rifle as the unfortunate animal staggered and lurched to the left. Race kicked his feet from the stirrups as his dying steed went over the edge of the trail and tumbled head over heels down the rocky slope, but it was closely followed by Race, his arms and legs flailing as he attempted to arrest his downward plunge.

Due to the steep angle of the slope there was no way he could arrest his progress, despite attempts to grasp at the bushes as he passed them. At one point his left foot became caught up between two large rocks and he stopped with a sickening jolt, suggesting that something in the limb might have snapped – but then his foot broke free and he continued rolling to the bottom of the slope, finally coming to rest alongside his dead horse.

Race lay there, half stunned and acutely aware of a sharp pain in his left ankle as the snow fell gently on his upturned face. Dimly, through narrowed eyes, he became aware of a dark figure high up the slope on the trail looking down on its handiwork – and Race realized that Bill Westerman had won this round.

CHAPTER FIFTEEN

The figure disappeared, satisfied no doubt that this time the corporal of the NWMP was well and truly dead, and that he was therefore free of any sort of pursuit – and Race was left to consider his own predicament.

The first thing he had to consider was some kind of shelter if these snow flurries turned into a true snowfall. Painfully he tried to stand up and look around his desolate location. He quickly determined that there were only trees, bushes and rocks of all shapes and sizes, and no sign of any human habitation – and for a brief moment his heart sank. Then he noticed through the trees that one of the forest giants, a huge pine, had fallen but had become lodged at forty-five degrees against its neighbours. There was a large cavity where the roots had been ripped from the earth, and Race decided that if he could get there, it was possible that it would provide shelter.

It was impossible to remove the saddle from the dead sorrel, but he did manage to untie the roll containing his duffle coat and also his waterproof slicker, together with some pigging strings, and the parcel of food provided by Joe Barton. Fortunately his canteen was on the side of the saddle that was uppermost, so he had no problem in retrieving it. Enduring sharp pain in his left foot at every step, Race hobbled the hundred and fifty yards that lay between his dead horse and possible sanctuary. Every step was pure agony, but gritting his teeth he made the distance, and sweating profusely, managed to reach the foot of the fallen pine tree.

Bending down he peered under the entangled mass of roots, earth and stones, and saw there was a space possibly four or five feet deep and six to eight feet in diameter, where the root system had been torn up by the falling tree. Thankfully it was as yet empty, and he didn't have to dispute ownership with some forest creature. Crouching, he crawled in and took possession of his new home.

Looking around in the half light he mentally shrugged his shoulders, thinking that things could be far worse. The cavity created by the fallen pine tree was dry, and the root system entangled with earth and all manner of small plants made a solid roof a couple of feet thick. Ferns and low shrubs had taken root around the cavity, and the falling snow was already banking up against these and thus protecting him from the effect of the wind inside his burrow.

He next took stock of his situation. There was little he could do during the snowstorm except try to keep dry and warm, and survive. He spread his slicker on the ground in an attempt to combat the dampness rising from the earth, and draped his duffle coat about his shoulders for additional warmth.

For a brief moment he had a rueful wish that he had the supplies packed on the little grey mare, but she, wise creature, had taken off like a rocket back towards Barton's Creek the moment her companion, the sorrel, had been shot. Coming back to reality Race sat and inspected the parcel of food Joe had given him as he was leaving Barton's Creek.

Joe had been very generous. Wrapped in tough brown paper and neatly tied, the food parcel contained half-a-dozen corn dodgers, several thick slices of cooked bacon, a hunk of strong-smelling cheese, four hard-boiled eggs and a good quarter of a loaf of home-baked bread. The saloon keeper of Barton's Creek intended to ensure the marshal did not starve. Together with the filled, untouched canteen of water Race considered he should be OK for several days, especially if he rationed his food carefully.

Although his left ankle throbbed unmercifully, a self-examination seemed to indicate that in fact he had survived his downhill tumble remarkably well. His clothing appeared untorn, and because his Colt was secured with a thong over the hammer, he had even retained his sidearm – not that he anticipated having to use it in the near future, unless some denizen of the wilds decided to take up residence in his new abode.

Reluctantly he made up his mind to check out his left foot, and carefully he unlaced and removed the riding boot and pulled off the long grey sock. Experimentally Race bent the left foot forward and tried to flex it in a circular movement. Each movement sent sharp pains up his lower leg and eventually he came to the conclusion that either some bone was broken or the ankle was internally torn and sprained.

The only treatment he could offer was to remove a sleeve from his shirt, thoroughly wet it in the snow and wrap it around the ankle, thus creating a cold compress. Having laboriously hauled his woollen sock over the compress, Race found that it was impossible to replace his riding boot so regretfully he left that off.

By now the light was beginning to fail and he realized that soon he would be faced with the long night of a northern location. Could he make a fire to create both light and heat? There were plenty of twigs, dead grass and leaves that had blown into the hollow, and with these he could certainly start a small fire. But could he sustain it through the night?

Race gathered some dead leaves and grass, making them into a little pile, and placed twigs around it as though making a child's tepee. Then taking one of his precious Lucifer 'strike anywhere' matches, he lit it and placed the burning match to the grass pile. It caught fire immediately, as did the dry twigs, and he had to hurriedly add more before the small blaze was completely consumed.

He needed more substantial material if he was going to keep the fire going, and breaking off one of the pine-tree roots hanging down inside his burrow, Race offered that to his fire. Being impregnated with resin the root burnt rapidly and he found that he had to replenish the fire frequently.

In addition to providing light the fire raised the temperature inside his shelter and Race found himself nodding off as he continued to feed his fire. He experimented with a root as thick as his wrist, putting one end in his fire and gradually advancing the piece as the root was burning. And so the strange night passed, with Race dozing in front of his fire and waking periodically to keep a steady blaze alight until daylight once more began to filter from the outside world into his burrow.

Outside it was still snowing, and Munro realized that with this weather, he wasn't going anywhere. He took one of the corn dodgers and hacked off a thick slice of bread, and making a home-made toasting fork from a slender elder shoot, he succeeded in browning both items over the fire; he then ate the crunchy results and washed them down with a swig of water.

While consuming his limited breakfast Race pondered over his predicament. There was the one possibility that the grey mare had run back as far as Barton's Creek and that her appearance had triggered a search party to set out looking for the missing law officer. Of course, such a party would no doubt have to wait until the weather improved before setting forth on such a venture – so he just had to be patient and wait.

On the other hand a nagging doubt gnawed at his sense of optimism. Supposing the mare didn't reach Barton's Creek? There were many carnivorous creatures including forest wolves, which would enjoy tearing to pieces a hapless horse astray in the wilderness. Or just supposing she fell in with some light-fingered fellow who would look upon the supplies she carried as manna from heaven. These notions and a dozen other possibilities ranged through Munro's mind as he tended his lonely fire.

He knew that to survive he had to remain positive that help was coming, or that the weather would improve sufficiently, and equally that his ankle would heal enough for him to make the trek back to Barton's Creek. In the meantime he set out to make things as comfortable as possible in an uncomfortable situation.

Race looked at the brown paper in which his provisions were wrapped, and a notion entered his head as he thought back to the pre-war days when as a boy, he had attended Dr Skinner's Academy for Young Gentlemen in far off Georgia. On one occasion the doctor had set out to prove to the class that it was possible to boil a cup of water in a paper bag.

Surely he, utilizing a square of the brown paper, could succeed in doing the same thing? Removing his provisions and placing them carefully on his slicker, Race spread out the brown paper and decided that he could remove a square of eight or nine inches and still have sufficient to re-wrap the food.

With the square thus obtained, he folded it diagonally corner to corner and then back, with each ear thus obtained until, racking his brain to recall the exact sequence of construction, he finally produced a receptacle capable of retaining water. Now, how could he improve on Dr Skinner's model? Piercing the paper at the thickest place on opposite sides of his receptacle, he used one of the pigging strings to create a handle, and a stout piece of aspen shoot to suspend his water container over the fire.

Immensely pleased that he had created a means of obtaining at least a small amount of warm or possibly hot water, Race sat back waiting for his 'kettle' to boil and celebrated his achievement by munching on another of the corn dodgers. Meanwhile the snow continued to fall, covering the land with a deep mantle of white.

Due to his culinary preparations and kettle making, Race had not thus far had any time to consider the condition of his left ankle, but he had noticed that the throbbing had diminished. At some time, which he figured was mid-afternoon, he decided that it was time to have an inspection, and so carefully he pulled off his sock and unwrapped the dried-out compress. With a minute quantity of warm water he washed the injured area and then spent a good ten minutes flexing the ankle and rotating the left foot, pointing it away from himself and then drawing it back, exercising the Achilles tendon.

Then he rewound the icy cold compress and replaced his sock, convinced that he had noticed a very slight improvement in his left ankle's condition.

The snow continued to fall for most of the day and banked up around the fallen pine tree, shutting out the light except for the place where Race had initially cleared away the undergrowth to gain entry to his refuge. There the snow had attempted to enter the hollow, but periodically he pushed it back and packed it so that his exit became smaller but he could still see the outside world. Fortunately, although the temperature was just below freezing, it had not plunged to the bone-chilling depths of mid-winter cold where bare skin could be severely frost bitten within five minutes of exposure.

Keeping his fire going and planning his next meal occupied Race's thoughts later in the day. He hung three or four strips of the bacon on a peeled stick over his fire, and putting the slightly charred results between two slabs of bread, consumed his sandwich with satisfaction, though regretting that he had not had the forethought to heat some water to accompany his supper.

As night fell the snow ceased completely and the wind also dropped. Race kept his fire banked up with the pine-tree roots and prepared to spend yet another night in his strange habitat.

Various thoughts flitted through his head as he sat there dozing over the flickering flames of his little fire.

By now Colonel French and his party of NWMP personnel must have reached Fort Benson and would have read the letter that he, Race, had left describing the murderous attack on the part of Trooper Westerman of Kurt Vogel and himself and the decision that he'd made to seek out the perpetrator. He hoped that the colonel understood his motive. Equally he hoped that Major Carson, the US commander of the Fort, had managed to obtain all the supplies required by the Canadian force, and also that he elaborated upon Race Munro's intentions.

Turning his mind back to the present he optimistically considered how soon it would be before Joe Barton could organize a search party to come seeking for him, always assuming that the little grey mare had reached Barton's Creek. He guessed that the following morning would be the earliest that they could set out, so he might well have to be patient and sit out most of the following day.

His thoughts regarding a rescue party would have been a great deal less positive if he had known what had transpired back at the Creek earlier that day. The mare had arrived in the early afternoon just as the snowfall began to fall steadily and was already drifting up on the porch of the saloon. Joe Barton, upon receiving word of the mare's arrival, had hurried out to see for himself the evidence that the marshal was probably having difficulties. Skidding on the wet, snow-covered boards of the porch he had fallen, striking his head, and was at that very moment lying

103

in bed suffering from severe concussion. There would be no hope of rescue from Barton's Creek until Joe recovered consciousness.

Unwillingly Race's thoughts turned to his would-be assassin. The late trooper had never struck Race as being over intelligent but rather a stolid, conscientious man, who would carry out a given order, but was not the type to initiate a plan of action. He, Race Munro, had sadly underestimated the man's ability to plan an ambush, which involved selecting a suitable site and waiting patiently in the cold for his victim to emerge within range of his rifle. Race surmised that the reason for his survival was probably the fact that Westerman had been shooting from a position high on the hill and had misjudged the amount that he had to aim higher to compensate for the fact that he was shooting downhill.

Where are you now Bill? Even if I have to follow you to Hell, Bill, I'm going to get you! And with that vow running through his head, Race Munro fell into an uneasy sleep.

CHAPTER SIXTEEN

Westerman, after gazing down the slope to where his victims, both man and horse, lay motionless two or three hundred feet below him, was more than satisfied with his morning's work, and moving to where his horse was hidden in a small gully, he mounted and rode swiftly towards the east.

Apart from periodic rests for his horse he kept moving all day, ignoring the snow which however seemed to lessen as he went further, especially as he began to change direction and eventually was headed towards the south.

It is said that the Devil helps his own, and that saying would certainly seem to be true in the case of Bill Westerman. Encountering the Musselshell River, which ran south, he was keeping the water on his left side, hoping that he would find some small hamlet where he could spend the night, when he was hailed from the bank. 'Hey stranger! Could you spare a couple of minutes to help this old coot wrastle this durned scow off of this mud bank?'

Now whether it was a pure quirk of circumstances or a remaining spark of decency manifesting itself within him, he responded in a neighbourly fashion, dismounting, securing his horse to a convenient bush, and scrambling down the bank with a cheery 'How can I help you, old-timer?'

'Wal, sonny!' the old boatman said, 'If you could just take this here pole an' use it to get leverage at the stern, that's that end, maybe I can free her up where her bow is nosing into the bank. It's the current, you see. The scow is too big for jus one man, an' my crew deserted. Took off after some female up at the last settlement. I figured that I could handle this stretch of the river alone, but I was wrong.'

While the elderly water rat was giving Westerman a running commentary on life on the river, the state of the economy and the problems of aging, they managed to get the large unwieldy scow parallel to the bank and securely moored ready for the next leg of its passage. It was then that the old boatman sprang his proposition upon Bill Westerman.

'Wal, I really appreciate you comin' to my aid. What did you say ya name was?' Bill volunteered that his name was Bill Webber, whereupon the elderly one introduced himself as Simeon Noshoes, Sim for short. He then made his suggestion.

'Wal Bill! I don't rightly know what your immediate plans are, but how would you like to hep' me get the *Gorgeous Girtie* down this durned river to Brownstown? It'll be the last run of the season before freeze up, and then I'll be hauling her out for the winter. You can bring that nag of yorn aboard – she'll be all right – and I'll give you fifty dollars for your assistance. That is, when I deliver this cargo!' he added hurriedly.

Bill didn't take many minutes to agree to the proposition. He was headed south. Sim would feed him on the voyage, and he would make a little bit of pocket money. If he didn't ease a great deal more out of the old water rat by the end of their association, he thought darkly.

His horse was brought aboard, trembling in this strange environment, and tethered amidships where a large bale of hay soon made her feel at home. Sim cast off the bow and stern lines, and the scow began to drift south, with Bill Webber handling the pole rudder that hung pivoted over the stern.

The wooden scow was a large, ungainly vessel, square at both ends and flat bottomed. The pole rudder was literally that: a long pole pivoted between two vertical upright posts. The lower end of the rudder had a slot milled in it, and in the slot were secured a number of three-feet long boards. When Bill pushed the rudder pole to the left the scow reluctantly swung from the bow to the right – or, as Sim insisted, to starboard. Conversely, moving the rudder the opposite way moved the front to the left – or, as the scow's owner stated emphatically, 'Moved the bow to port!'

Apart from the disagreement over nautical and landlubbers' shipping terms, the crew were quite amicable. Bill did most of the steering. The river did most of the pushing, and all Sim had to do was to stand in the bow fending off obstacles such as tree trunks going in the same general direction, and warn of the approaching danger in the shape of rocks and muddy shallows.

Each evening the scow was drawn into the river bank and Sim set to work cooking their supper on a stone slab amidships. After the meal, which was generally stew, the crew sat and smoked their pipes for a short while before turning in under the primitive lean-to, which provided shelter in the event of adverse weather.

As the days passed old Sim became more and more communicative, telling a story of a hard childhood in a fishing port on the east coast, and later employment on the Ohio and the mighty Mississippi rivers. He spoke of the gang warfare and the skulduggery that occurred, of vessels sunk or burnt in the night, or of crew members who suddenly vanished without trace. But those were the bad old days, said Sim. On these western rivers you just have to contend with Mother Nature and the constant thieving habits of the native population.

Bill Webber just sat there and said very little about himself or his past, until finally one day Sim said: 'Heh Bill! You don't have too much to add to the conversation, do you?' Then he posed the question, 'Are you on the dodge or something? You seem to be always lookin' over your shoulder!'

There was a long sigh and finally Bill Webber gave a theatrical sigh. 'Well, Sim, I guess I'd better tell you the whole story.

'I'd been away from home working and came back to find my little – well, she's not so little – sister was in a whole mess of trouble. She'd taken up with some local fella, and he'd got our Bella in the family way.

'Ma was all upset over the affair and wouldn't speak to Bella. Pa, even though he'd threatened to drive my sister from the house, relented, but said he intended if that Bert Alonzo came near the property he'd let fly with his old ten-gauge scattergun. Poor Pa, he was so badly wounded fighting for the Union he couldn't really do anything.

'So one day that Alonzo fella came up to the front door as bold as brass, stating that our Bella owed him twenty dollars and he wanted his money. Bella of course denied it. Dad outs with his scattergun and Bert pulls his pistol. Before he could level it at Pa I drew mine and ordered him to drop his Colt. Instead of following my suggestion he turned his gun towards me with the avowed intention of shooting me. But I fired first and hit him plumb in the bread basket. My shot, I tell ya, was self-defence.

'Unfortunately Bert died, and since his brother was the local marshal he stirred up the folks against me. There was no chance of a fair trial. They just wanted to string me up, so I lit out and I've been on the dodge for the past two months.'

Sim commiserated with Bill Webber over his sad story of a young woman betrayed and about the miscarriage of justice. Then he posed a practical question, 'Bill, you've got ta get out of Montana territory until somehow you can clear your name. What are you going to do during the winter months?'

Bill Westerman, to give him his original surname, didn't answer, but just sat there pondering the question. He could hardly express what was going through his mind, which was to kill the old man and steal whatever he could get for the scow and its cargo.

Sim, taking his silence as an indication that Bill was waiting for him to make a suggestion, decided to break the silence between them.

'What you need, boy, is a safe place where you can hole up for the winter months and nobody is going to question your past. You, like many a man before you, are on the owl-hoot trail, where every man you meet is an enemy unless proven otherwise. Now, on the trail there are certain places where a fella can hole up and nobody will ask any questions.

'One is Robbers' Roost, but that's down in Utah territory and its location is a hell of a ride from here. Another safe hideout is in Wyoming Territory. It's an isolated location known as the Hole in the Wall – there's a few cabins and shanties, and everyone present chips in to stock the food and the grub. It's secure. How do I know that? Well, Bill, I've done many things in my life beside handling boats, an' I've bin to the

Hole a couple of times. But first thing that you've got to do is get rid of that military holster. Cut the flap off otherwise folks may get the idea you could be a government agent and dispose of you. They won't take any chances.'

Bill Westerman was in a dilemma. On the one hand he could easily get rid of Sim and go merrily on his way. On the other hand, having a guide to a secure winter refuge sounded pretty good, and maybe he could fall in with some like-minded gents. He decided to be duly grateful and therefore he accepted Sim's offer of assistance and obeyed his instructions to the letter.

Following the old water rat's directions, Bill made his way south into Wyoming Territory, avoiding towns and stopping only at isolated ranches and lonely cabins, where the owners greeted him gruffly yet asked no questions as to where he came from nor where he was headed, as long as he included the word 'Hole' in the opening conversation.

Several days of hard riding later, he and his weary bronc made their way up a rocky, little used trail towards the wall of red frowning cliffs that stretched to the horizon to both his left and his right. The trail led to where a narrow cleft gave entry through the wall of rock and into the isolated valley that lay beyond.

Down in the valley several hundred feet below were a few signs of human habitation. He could see a fair-sized cabin with smoke curling up from a chimney, haphazardly surrounded by a number of smaller buildings – shanties or more probably soddies.

Relieved that his weary journey appeared to be nearing its end Bill Westerman was about to urge his horse to take the trail down to the settlement below when he froze as a voice cried out; 'Hold it right there fella. Let's you an' me have a little pow-wow before you go where maybe you're not wanted.'

CHAPTER SEVENTEEN

Race woke up shivering as the pale light of the early sunlight entered his root shelter. His fire had burnt down to practically nothing, and he was cold, stiff and hungry, with the inside of his mouth feeling furred and distinctly unpleasant.

He scrabbled around seeking the last vestiges of dried grass and a few overlooked leaves with which to restart his fire, with the sober thought that if no rescue party arrived on that day he was going to be in dire straits indeed.

By careful rationing he figured that he could make his food last for another two days, but fresh water was certainly going to be a major problem. Shaking his canteen and examining the contents, he estimated that it still held less than a cup full of water, and he started stuffing snow into the container – though fully realizing that a large quantity of snow was required to create only a very small amount of liquid.

Race broke his fast with the last of the corn dodgers as he waited for his near collapsing paper 'kettle' to heat a small quantity of water, both to slake his thirst and to bathe his ankle after an examination and his attempts at exercise.

As he was completing the check of his injured limb and assuring himself that even if it was no better, it certainly appeared no worse, he heard a familiar sound up on the trail above: the clip-clopping of horses' hoofs on the stony surface of the mountain trail. From the multiple sounds it appeared to be several horses, and his hopes rose as he realized that rescue could be close at hand.

Drawing his Colt, he fired two shots into the ground – the conventional method of attracting attention – and the grey smoke from the two explosions billowed around inside his shelter and curled up into the outside air.

The noise of the horses' hoofs had ceased with the sound of the pistol shots and Race waited, hoping that he had attracted attention. Minutes passed and finally he heard the welcome sound of feet crunching through the snow. He called out: 'Hello there! I'm here, under the pine tree!'

There was silence, and then moments later the light inside Race's burrow was blocked out as a dark figure on its hands and knees peered in at him, and a deep, guttural voice said: 'How!'

Race, realizing that his visitor was an Indian, responded with a similar greeting and went on to briefly relate how his horse had been shot and he had crawled under the uprooted pine to shelter during the snowstorm.

The Indian brave remained silent during Race's description, apart from the odd 'Ugh' of approval or disapproval during the narrative. When Race had finished the Indian said; 'Me Young Horse. You?'

To which the white man replied, 'My name is Munro. Race Munro.' But before he could express his thanks for the anticipated rescue, Young Horse excitedly broke in on Race's discourse. 'You are Mun-ro? The man who makes Whites obey the law? Then we are friends, not strangers. We must get you to our lodge. This place is not good. Smells like badger.'

Race was inclined to agree that his current habitation left a great deal to be desired when it came to waste disposal, and rubbing his hand across his face, realized that while thus entombed he had started the growth of a scratchy beard.

Together they enlarged the entrance and Race crawled out and stood up, steadied by Young Horse. The latter called out, and two other braves slipped down from the trail above and proceeded to clear away the snow from Race's dead horse in order to retrieve his rifle, saddle and saddlebags. While they were thus engaged Young Horse explained in broken English why Mun-ro was known to him and his people.

'We are Hunkpapas of the Lakota, the people you Whites call Sioux. You helped my Grandfather, Sitting Bull, when he had problems with bad Whites.

115

You also helped Rosebud. She is my sister and speaks very well of the marshal they call Mun-ro.'

Young Horse, seeing the difficulty that Race had standing, let alone walking on his damaged ankle, gave him a piggyback ride up the mountain side to where the Lakota horses were waiting. Two of the young Lakota braves rode double, while a third carried Race's saddle and impedimenta, since none of the Lakota horses had ever been saddled, leaving one of the ponies free for him to ride with just a blanket for comfort. Luckily, Race had excelled at the depot of the NWMP in riding bare-back during the recruit training, before commencing the long march to the West, and so he did not experience too much of an ordeal in riding in this fashion. It was with a heart-felt sense of relief that he looked down for one last glance at what had been his temporary home.

As they rode, Young Horse told Race something about his people, their background and the problems that they were currently facing. He described how the Hunkpapa Lakota were related to other Sioux tribes including the Oglala, Miniconjou, Brule, Sans Arc, the Blackfoot and the Arapaho. How at one time they had been spread all over the plains and even up into the area the Whites called Canada.

Originally they had been crop growers, but when they acquired horses from their cousins the Northern Cheyenne, increasingly they became mounted hunters. But then the Whites came in ever increasing numbers, pushing westwards and driving the people of the plains back from their traditional hunting grounds. White migration followed, and when the government in Washington decided to build a string of forts to protect what they called the Bozeman Trail across traditional Sioux territory, the tribes under chief Red Cloud went to war.

After a number of military setbacks and at least one disaster, the Americans had called for peace treaty talks. Red Cloud had agreed, and the two sides had hammered out an agreement.

The military would dismantle the forts erected along the Bozeman Trail, and the Lakota promised that settlers travelling to the west could use that route without fear of attack. Another important clause was that the area in Dakota and Montana territory known as the Black Hills would be forever Lakota land, and no Whites would ever be permitted to settle there.

Young Horse looked at Race and smiled grimly: 'Now soldiers, led by the one they call Custer, have come to our sacred hills. They have found the yellow metal you Whites call gold, and they say they want our land. The people are very angry that the Whites do not keep their word after making an agreement with the Lakota. I do not know what will happen, but many are calling for war.

'But do not fear, Mun-ro. You are a friend of Lakota, and Sitting Bull he say you will always be safe in our lodge because you punished the bad Whites.'

The terrain through which they were riding consisted in the main of rolling hills with wide, grass-covered valleys, while the slopes of the uplands were covered with varied arboreal growth, which from a distance produced an overall dark appearance – hence the name 'the Black Hills'.

In one location known as the valley of the greasy grass a large Lakota encampment could be seen, and presently the little cavalcade was riding through large numbers of horses that were the responsibility of a dozen young boys, one of whom threw himself on his pony and raced off to the village upon seeing a white man with the approaching party.

His announcement brought out numbers of mounted braves who rode around Race and his group brandishing rifles, carbines and even the odd musket, and yelling what were apparently hostile remarks. Race, remembering his NWMP training, sat up straight and stared ahead, doing his best to ignore the visual threats hurled in his direction. Young Horse intervened, roaring at the milling crowd to back off and to behave with courtesy towards the friend and guest of his grandfather, Sitting Bull.

At that name the excitable mob fell silent and one could sense an evident embarrassment with the realization that they had behaved badly towards an honoured guest.

Young Horse and his group halted before a big tepee, in front of which a stately figure was standing, and beside him a small slender form that Race immediately recognized. It was Rosebud, who smiled a welcome to him, though she stood back demurely as befitting a Lakota maid as her grandfather Sitting Bull stepped forwards to greet the white man.

Sitting Bull delivered a lengthy address, which Young Horse translated with some difficulty into English. 'My grandfather he say he is very happy to see Mun-ro, and he welcomes you to share his lodge and all that is his. He also say that he is sorry that you have had bad fortune and a broken foot and he hopes we can make it well again.'

Race bowed his head gravely and expressed his thanks to Sitting Bull for being so generous with his hospitality, and apologized that under the circumstances he was unable to come bearing gifts, as was befitting.

Young Horse delivered Race's response to Sitting Bull and the latter looked pleased and gestured for the visitor to dismount. Race did so, but stood in obvious discomfort, bearing his weight on his right foot while his left toes barely touched the ground.

'Young Horse, could you explain to your grandfather that I would like to clean up before I accept his very kind invitation.'

The Lakota brave did as requested, whereupon Sitting Bull issued a number of orders in rapid succession; Race then found himself being administered to in ways he was not accustomed to. Two brawny young men picked him up and carried him bodily to a small, empty tepee and deposited him inside upon a buffalo hide. His saddlebags followed, and then suddenly the tepee was invaded by several Lakota women, who, ignoring his protests, proceeded to strip him of all his clothing until he was buck naked. Race's protests were in vain as he attempted to retain a few shreds of modesty.

Two more women entered carrying a large leather bucket of steaming water, and they proceeded to wash him from head to toe, laughing and chattering back and forth about the uniqueness of his white skin while they bathed him.

When he had been thoroughly washed and dried and wrapped in a Hudson's Bay blanket, a very old Lakota woman came into the tepee; the others fell back respectfully as she patted him on the shoulder, and kneeling down examined his left ankle with gentle deft fingers. At length the old woman –whose Lakota title was 'Mother of the people' – took from a bag a strip of softened leather covered in cabalistic signs, and wrapped it around Race's left ankle, singing quietly to herself as she did so. Then for a good five minutes there was complete silence in the tepee as she just sat there with one hand resting lightly on Race's ankle.

Suddenly she unwrapped the strange bandage, and smiling a toothless look of encouragement at her white patient, told him through Young Horse that his ankle would be completely cured in three moons – that is, three days. Her mission accomplished, she rose painfully to her feet and shuffled from the tepee.

Race was baffled by his experience. Something had happened in the tepee that was far beyond his ken, and he did not know what to make of it. Certainly his injured ankle felt better, and eventually he just decided to accept what had happened as a strange occurrence.

Thanking the 'ladies' for their assistance, he stood and shooed them from the tepee; then he hurriedly delved into his saddlebags and found a pair of red 'long johns' underpants, which he swiftly donned, followed by a clean pair of jeans and a tartan checked shirt. Once fully dressed he removed the contents from his forcibly discarded clothing, and asked Young Horse if one of the women would wash them and hang them up to dry. This was done – and Race felt that finally he was getting organized.

With an appreciable limp Race stepped out from the tepee and looked around. Young Horse wasn't to be seen, and he felt isolated, being unable to communicate with the many Lakota going about their normal activities and trying to behave as though it was a normal situation to have a white man living in the village.

CHAPTER EIGHTEEN

As he stood there undecided as to what was the correct thing for a guest to do, a small figure sidled up to him and slipped a warm hand into his.

'Good day to you, Marshal Munro. I was beginning to think that you had forgotten the girl who sewed up and dressed the knife wound in your back not so long ago.'

'Rosebud!' Race turned to behold the smiling face of the Lakota girl looking impishly up at him, and instinctively he pulled her towards him and hugged her fiercely, saying, 'This is probably against all the rules of Lakota hospitality, but lass, am I glad to see you! Your brother has been acting as interpreter for me, but suddenly he's disappeared and I'm standing here lost.'

'Young Horse has to resume his normal role, which is that of hunter. Most of the young men at this time of the year are busy hunting, securing food that can be preserved to last the clan through the winter.'

Rosebud looked at Race solemnly. 'With Young Horse absent, somebody had to look after you and make sure that you are being cared for, and my grandfather told me that this is to be my responsibility. Have you eaten yet?'

Race stated that apart from a piece of dried meat chewed on during the long ride to the Lakota camp, he had consumed nothing since his early breakfast in the pine tree shelter. 'Now that you mention it, young lady, I'm beginning to feel decidedly hungry! What time is supper?'

Rosebud laughed, and explained that in fact she had been delegated to bring Munro to the big tepee to dine with Sitting Bull and several of the other Lakota dignitaries. But she suggested that Race remove his gun-belt and leave his Colt in the small tepee. Such a gesture would please her grandfather and show that he felt at home in the Lakota village.

Race did as she suggested, and then, leaning heavily on Rosebud's shoulder, he limped slowly over to the large tepee where Sitting Bull and a number of the other chiefs were assembled.

Sitting Bull greeted Race warmly, and then introduced the dozen or so solemn guests seated in a circle around a smouldering fire. As he announced each one, Rosebud translated their names into English for the benefit of the white man – and thus he came to know Crazy Horse, War Chief of the Oglala, Little Wolf and Dull Knife of the Northern Cheyenne, and Chief

Gall of the Lakota. There were others, of course, but it was impossible to remember all the names.

When Race gave a hearty 'Howdy' to each introduction, most responded with a muttered 'How', except for Crazy Horse, who sat with lips pursed, merely glaring at the white intruder.

As a guest of honour Race was invited to sit next to Sitting Bull on his right side, and then a succession of Lakota women entered, bringing dishes for each of the guests. Rosebud knelt behind Race as he became the possessor of three small bowls, and as a special concession a small iron spoon, evidently of European origin.

The bowls were filled, and Rosebud endeavoured to explain to Race the nature of each course. The meal started with a mush of corn, which had been removed from the cob and boiled with chopped mushrooms and herbs. This was followed by wild rice cooked with dried berries and herbs. In the middle of the dish was a small ball of pemmican consisting of dried buffalo meat pounded almost to a powder and mixed with an equal quantity of thick, almost tallow animal fat and herbs and berries.

Race was beginning to feel comfortably full when the ladies appeared once more, this time with a big iron pot containing a thick meat stew, which Rosebud hastened to assure Race was made with venison and not, as sometimes happened, with dog meat.

Eating was a serious business with these gentlemen, and the dinner conversation was limited in the main to grunts of satisfaction as Lakota bellies were filled to satisfaction. To Race's surprise the meal ended with each guest receiving a small tin cup of thick black coffee, which had apparently been brought to the village by Sitting Bull when he returned from his journey during which the White yahoos had been so offensive.

With the meal ended a ceremonial pipe was produced, and after Sitting Bull had inhaled the initial smoke, the pipe was passed clockwise around the circle, with each smoker uttering grunts of satisfaction as they completed their pull on the coarse native tobacco.

Race, being on Sitting Bull's right, was the last to receive the pipe, and as his turn drew nearer, he looked forward with no little apprehension to the notion of placing the spittle-laden stem anywhere near his lips. His turn arrived, and he took the long pipe with his left hand holding the bowl while his clenched right hand formed a funnel around the stem, thus keeping the latter a good half inch from his lips as he inhaled heartily and exhaled with obvious satisfaction.

The post-dinner conversation focused on the white intrusion into the Black Hills, which the American government by treaty had promised would be Lakota land forever. The white gold miners were ravaging the land in their mad search for the yellow metal, and the Lakota people were rapidly being driven from their traditional territory.

Coupled with this was the realization that the buffalo, from which since time immemorial they had obtained food, shelter and clothing, and had had many other uses, was diminishing rapidly. Gone were the vast herds that covered the land from east to west in the course of their annual migrations, and travellers reported that to the south could be seen countless carcases of the beasts, killed for their hides alone – the rest of the animals, apart from the hump and the tongue, had been left to rot, making the land stink with their putrefaction.

Sitting Bull held up his hand for silence and then spoke at great length to Rosebud, and Race knew that at least some of the remarks referred to himself, since he identified the word 'Munro' repeated several times. The chief finished, and Rosebud stood up, motioning for Race to do the same.

'We have to leave,' she whispered. 'Just thank my grandfather for his hospitality and quickly bid the whole group goodnight, and then we must depart.'

Race did as he was instructed, and then the two of them left the tepee. Race was very anxious to know why his host had suddenly decided that the guest of honour was no longer welcome, and to hear Rosebud's explanation and the gist of Sitting Bull's long talk to her. He therefore suggested they take a little stroll together, and she could then enlighten him.

'It's quite simple, really, Race. The chiefs had been discussing the perils facing the Lakota people, and with maybe the exception of Gall, they had decided that the only answer is to fight to retain the Black Hills. Going to war with the American government is a very serious business, and Grandfather believed that, despite the fact that you are a friend, being white, the least you know, the better it is for you.'

Race remained silent while he digested Rosebud's information and its implications for him. As a white man he would obviously be expected, not only by the Lakota but also by the American authorities, to side with his own race in any forthcoming strife. But it was not the sort of complicated situation that he had anticipated when he took on the role of a Montana Territory marshal.

For a short while he said nothing as, ignoring his limp and the light snowfall covering the ground, they walked slowly towards the outskirts of the Lakota village, acknowledging the friendly waves of individuals and families engaged in their evening pursuits. Finally he turned to Rosebud, and grasping her by the upper arms, looked deep into her eyes and said: 'Rosebud, my dear, how much can I trust you with a big secret?'

Rosebud looked up at him, and shaking her head in mock dismay declared: 'Marshal Race Munro! Of course you can trust me with any secret. Surely you know that, although we have not known each other for a very long time, there is some kind of magic between us? Can you not feel it, Race?'

Race pulled her close to him and lightly kissed her on the forehead. 'Yes, dear girl, I think I've known it since the moment that we first met, but I've hesitated to put this feeling into words in case I offended you, or broke some Lakota taboo – but now listen carefully.

'First of all, I am not an American. That is, I still don't swear loyalty to the United States government in Washington. I suppose if I'm anything I guess I'm a Canadian, since I took an oath of obedience to Queen Victoria.'

Rosebud looked at him in amazement. 'Are you then a soldier of the Great White Queen who rules the lands to the north? How can this be?'

Race decided to start at the beginning and told her how originally he had been a 'Gray Rider' serving the Confederate states and had been sent up to Canada on a military mission. He described the years in Ontario after the end of the Civil War, and how he had enlisted in the North West Mounted Police and had taken part in the great march west.

He continued with an account of his mission to Fort Benson, the murderous treachery of Bill Westerman, and the death of Kurt Vogel; his decision to hunt down Westerman, and his subsequent adventures posing as Marshal Munro; ending with the shooting of his horse and his arrival in the Lakota village.

'I see my first duty as being to avenge the death of young Vogel, and the capture or killing of Westerman. My second duty is to provide Colonel French with my long overdue report regarding the advance patrol that he sent to Fort Benson.

'Although I deeply sympathize with the Lakota and firmly believe that they have been treated unjustly by the American government, I could not join them in a war against the whites. Equally, I would not join the white soldiers fighting against the Lakota. I would just stay neutral unless I saw a situation where either side was intent on creating a bloodbath, in which case I might have to intervene.'

Race and Rosebud decided to keep the details of their evening disclosures to themselves, and also their declared feeling for each other, in the hope that the situation for the people would improve in the spring and that Race would get his man. In the meantime he would continue to live in the village, assisting where he could, and gathering information regarding the whereabouts of the renegade that he sought.

CHAPTER NINETEEN

Bill Westerman sat rigid on his weary horse as first one, and then a second rifle-toting character appeared from between the rocks and quartered him between their potential cross-fire. The riflemen approached and eyed him up and down with the utmost suspicion.

'Wal fella, what's yer handle, an' what's yer excuse for riding this trail?' The one who challenged him, a bearded character sporting a yellow kerchief as part of a once expensive jacket and pants that were now merely sad remnants of former splendour, raised his weapon menacingly as he demanded an instant reply.

'Name's Webber! Bill Webber! I've come a whole lot of miles to find this hole in the wall, an' I'm sure there'll be a welcome for a poor traveller on the dodge who just wants to find shelter for the winter.'

The bearded one opened his mouth and guffawed, revealing a mouth with broken, tobacco-stained teeth.

'Hee hee! That sure is a mighty fine reason why a body might be seeking a place by the fire. What'cha say Amos? Do yer figure that this 'ere Bill Webber qualifies to join us for the winter, or shall we send 'im to a warmer place?'

'Naw Tom!' This from his companion, a little runt of a man dressed in an assortment of cast-off clothing yet wielding a heavy Sharps rifle in immaculate condition. ''E's all right. 'E's familiar wiv the password, and we 'ad to look aht for a bloke name of Webber.'

Amos Smith's mangling of the English language revealed his trans-Atlantic origin, but Westerman was glad that he was more affable than his fellow guard. The two on guard duty argued back and forth for several minutes until they both finally agreed that Bill Webber probably didn't represent a threat to the community, and after firing a single shot to announce that a newcomer was on his way, they indicated that he could proceed.

Riding with care he negotiated the steep mountain trail that led down into the wide, closed valley that constituted the 'hole in the wall'. The track began to level out as he reached the bottom of the decline, and he was able to take his eyes off the pathway and experience more interest in the small settlement that he was approaching.

The word 'settlement' was indeed too strong a term to describe the single large cabin and the half-dozen smaller structures that made up the community, rather like baby chicks huddling close to their mother hen. These satellite dwellings were sod houses with walls made of turf, with boards laid across to form a roof and with more turf on top to hold the boards down. The crude entrances had doors roughly nailed together and held in place with hinges made from strips of leather. Pieces of galvanized piping from which there came eddies of smoke indicated that at least two 'soddies' had some form of heating.

With the sober thought that one of these earthen structures would no doubt be his 'home sweet home', Bill Westerman rode to the main cabin, dismounted, and tied his horse to the hitching rail. Then drawing his Snider from its saddle boot, he headed for the cabin door with his loaded long gun cradled in his left arm.

Pushing open the door he stepped in quickly, then stopped to survey the interior of the main room and the assembled company. The room was about thirty feet square with an L-shaped bar across the back wall. In the centre of the room was a large, pot-bellied stove that was glowing a dull red in places and sending forth a goodly amount of heat, enough for most of those present to have shed their outer garments.

Westerman nodded a greeting and a loud 'Howdy' to all present, and stepped forwards to where a portly bearded man stood waiting silently behind the counter.

'Webber's the name, Bill Webber! I understand that you can provide me with lodgings and food and drink as long as I pay my whack.' He reached into a pocket and produced four twenty gold-piece double eagles, and slapped them down on the counter.

'There's eighty dollars, which I figure should cover most of my bill, according to what Sim Noshoes told me,' and he waited for the other to make a response.

'Well, thankee kindly, Bill. That'll all go in the general pot. That's the way we do things here. We fix two meals a day, a breakfast which is always the same biscuit and gravy, same as many fellas is used to, then in late afternoon or early evening we fix a decent sized dinner with meat an' 'taters, whatever vegetables is going, an' bread or biscuits an' sometimes dumplings. An' of course there's always coffee. The bar is open after dinner 'til close on midnight. But you'll have to pay for your liquor.

'My name's Leo Krangston, by the way, but most of the fellas call me Pop since I seem to be acting as father to the lot of them at times.

'Now! You'll need somewhere to kip. How did you get on with those two lads up on the guard post? All right, you say. That's good, because they have one spare bunk in their soddy, an' that's where you'll be kipping. First soddy across the road from the cookhouse here. Can't miss it. Old Amos Smith has scratched what he calls a Union Jack on the door. Dunno why! Anyhow, that's how you'll recognize it.

'Turn your nag into the large corral behind the cookhouse. Someone will toss in a bundle of hay for the critturs there.

'OK, Bill Webber. I've said my piece! Now off you go and get settled in, there'll be grub on the table about sundown! See you then!' And Pop Krangston turned away as Bill took his Snider from the counter and left the cookhouse; he turned his horse loose, having removed both saddle and blanket, and sought his winter quarters.

The soddy, with smoke curling from its improvised stovepipe chimney, was exactly as Leo Krangston had described it, with a crudely depicted British Union Jack scratched deeply into the door panel. Seeing the emblem under which he had grown up, and which he had promised to serve faithfully, sent a qualm of guilt shivering through Webber, but he sternly rejected the feeling, and pushing the door open wide, he stepped inside.

He stood for a moment allowing his eyes to become accustomed to the pale interior light provided by a hole in the left-hand side of the soddy, into which some enterprising character had stuck a piece of glass in lieu of a window. That, and because at that moment the door was open, enabled Westerman to gain familiarity with his new home.

The soddy was roughly square in shape, about twelve feet per side. On the side facing the door was a bunk with tumbled blankets, obviously belonging to one of his fellow residents, and the left-hand bunk beneath the solitary 'window' was in a similar state. The bunk on the right was empty of all possessions, and was obviously his, once he had dumped his horse blanket and saddle on the bare chicken-wire frame to claim occupancy. He noted two or three pegs driven into the sod wall above the bunk from which he could hang his clothing, and once he had placed his saddle at the end of the bunk to act as a pillow, and spread his blanket on the wire frame, he began to feel at home.

The home-made stove producing the smoke he had observed earlier was to the left of the doorway, and consisted of no more than a large metal box on its side, to which some budding heating engineer had wired a length of galvanized stove piping and likewise a door. The draught to draw the fire was provided by holes punched in the sides of the box, and a pile of small branches indicated the fuel supply.

Using his kerchief as a glove he opened the door of the stove and fed the smouldering embers with some pieces from the pile. Then shutting the door of the soddy he rolled a cigarette and lay down on his bunk and rested.

He had hardly finished his cigarette when the sound of hoofs was heard, and shortly after, the creak of leather and a jingle of harness as horses were unsaddled. There was a mutter of voices and the door was opened, and Amos Smith staggered in under the weight of his saddle and long gun.

He tottered over to the bunk opposite the door, and noticing the recumbent form, dropped his gear and turned to Westerman with a cheery greeting: 'Watcha, me old cock sparrer! So Pop put you in wiv us, eh? Well, I must say you're more'n welcome.

Amos Smiff's me moniker. Born in Stepney, London, but I's bin in these United States more years an' I care to remember.'

Further enlightening details of Amos's past were interrupted by the bearded fellow from the guard post who, having turned their horses into the corral, now sought the shelter of his soddy.

Amos genially introduced his bearded partner to Bill Westerman, saying, 'This 'ere's me best friend, Tom Warner! 'E's a good friend to 'ave in a fight, but don't lend 'im nuffink because you ain't likely to get it back!'

Tom Warner shook hands with Bill, who introduced himself as Webber and smiled when the former growled and commented, 'Don't believe anything this Limey runt tells you. He'd sell his own grandmother if he could get a good price for her!'

The good-natured bantering went on between the two bunk mates until eventually Amos declared that it was time to head over to the cookhouse for the evening meal – at which suggestion the stove was banked up and the trio went over to the main cabin.

The food was laid out along the counter of the bar, and the men, each grabbing a plate and utensils, moved along shovelling potatoes, stew and vegetables on to their plates from the steaming cooking pots. Then adding biscuits to their fare they sought empty spaces at the tables and benches where they could consume the evening meal.

Bill Webber was introduced to others at the table, and they responded with a curt 'Howdy' or a quick nod as they applied themselves to the task of emptying their plates.

It was as the meal was in progress that he saw a different side of Amos Smith, his room-mate. One of the neighbours at the table chose a moment when Amos's attention was distracted away from his plate, to slide it completely out of reach at the end of the long table. When Amos's eyes returned from their distraction to behold a bare place where previously his evening dinner had resided, he flew into a terrible rage. ''Ere, what's this? What thievin' bastard has pinched me grub? 'And it over or it'll be grief fer someone!'

Bill Webber was never exactly sure what happened next. The man on Amos's right said something and raised his left arm as though to threaten the little Londoner. There was a sudden flash of light upon steel, and the man jumped up cursing as he clutched at this arm, which was pouring blood.

Amos also stood, waving an open razor back and forth before his victim's eyes and threatening to cut him to ribbons. Pop and a number of those present intervened, calming the enraged Britisher, while others administered first aid to the injured party.

Amos returned his folded razor to an open pocket of his jacket, and in a calm voice explained what had caused the outburst. 'When 'e took me dinner I was angry, but when 'e said nasty fings about me muvver,

137

that made me blow me top. 'E said she was on the game, which she was, but 'e 'ad no cause to insult 'er. She was a good muvver to me an' no mistake, so I let 'im 'ave it.'

Bill Webber, impressed by Amos's filial devotion to his no doubt long-departed mother, decided that in this establishment it was wiser to keep a still tongue in one's head. And he went to bed that night unsure of how he was going to survive through the winter months.

CHAPTER TWENTY

Race Munro rather enjoyed the unique experience of fitting in as an adopted member of a Hunkpapa lodge, which was brightened considerably by the constant presence of Rosebud. He had his meals with the family, and initially retired at night to the small tepee set aside for visitors. It wasn't long, however, before he moved his gear over to the large tepee and was accepted as one of the family.

As he had been told by the Wise Woman, his ankle was fully healed in three days, and he found that it would bear his weight without any discomfort. Race was pleased, yet curious, when Sitting Bull called for him early one morning saying, 'Come walk with me, Munro, I would have your advice.' Race walked with the old chief, wondering why he, of all people, could be expected to give advice to one so sage in the councils of the Lakota.

In an open space a lovely roan mare was tethered, and as they drew near, Sitting Bull said, 'Tell me Munro, what do you think of this animal?'

139

Race walked around the mare studying all its good points and not finding any negative aspects to remark upon. Holding it by the halter he carefully examined the mare's strong yellow teeth and found no evidence of disease. Finally he turned to Sitting Bull and stated this indeed was a mighty fine animal, at which the chief smiled, and said, ''Good! It is good that you like her. She is yours now. A gift from the Lakota.' And thus Race Munro was given a replacement for the horse that had been shot on the mountain trail weeks earlier.

The days passed and the snow fell more and more frequently. The Lakota spent much of the time huddled inside their individual dwellings, each with a fire continually burning to ward off the cold of the outside air. The waking hours were mainly spent in repairing hunting equipment and continually servicing the few guns that the village possessed, eating, talking, and telling stories. After a while Race found that he had acquired a smattering of Lakota words and terms, and could join in the jocular repartee that the other members were engaged in.

He had told Sitting Bull of his quest to find the man who had killed Kurt Vogel, and had even attempted to murder him, and the chief had caused the word to be spread, so that when spring finally arrived and people started to travel once more, information would be received if a man answering Westerman's description left the safety of the hole in the wall, where he was believed to be hiding.

Race heard no more of the talk among the Lakota to make war upon the white soldiers and settlers who were despoiling the tribes of their land, but he noticed that if there were strangers in the camp people would fall silent when he drew near, and would then talk loudly of commonplace things as though to reassure him that their conversations were innocent.

But there was one curious incident that aroused his suspicions. One sunny day when the temperature rose above freezing and people wondered if spring was in the air, a strange uncouth white man arrived on the outskirts of the village mounted on a black horse and leading two pack animals.

Race was standing at the entry to the large tepee talking to Sitting Bull, and directly the stranger came into view the wily chief said, 'Munro, come in here – I must talk seriously with you.'

Race of course went in, though in truth he would like to have remained and seen what cargo the stranger was carrying. He sat down facing Sitting Bull, who spoke long and lovingly about his granddaughter, known to Munro as Rosebud. He described her birth, her childhood, and her growth into the lovely young woman that she was today, and outlined all her skills and qualities, which made her such an attractive proposition as a potential wife to any man lucky enough to win her affections.

Sitting Bull droned on for at least two hours and Race listened politely, although, frequently, he found the soporific murmuring of the old Hunkpapa chief was lulling

141

him into a drowsy state. Suddenly there was an inter-ruption. One of the braves that Race only knew by sight entered and spoke to the chief, far too swiftly for the white man to follow. Sitting Bull immediately rose, while motioning for Race to remain seated and left the tepee while the unknown brave remained by the entrance. To Race he didn't seem hostile, but merely impassive, standing there with his rifle cradled in his arms.

And that rifle he carried was the second thing that Race noticed. The Hunkpapas, with whom he had been in contact for several weeks now, mostly sported older, single-shot rifles of the Remington rolling-block type, with the occasional 1866 Henry lever-action repeater firing a rimfire .44 round. But the brave in front of him had one of the new 1873 Winchesters, which fired a more potent 44.40 centre-fire cartridge. A large force of hostile Lakota armed with repeating rifles could pose a serious problem for any military forces sent against them by the US Government.

Race made a mental note to himself to pass on the news about the repeating rifles to his friend Major Carson at Fort Benson when finally he was head-ing north. The news might save a few lives if strife occurred between the Lakota and the US military.

As the days passed there was no mention of the white trader who had visited the village, nor of the guns that had appeared and subsequently disap-peared. There were, however, other excitements.

Race was sitting outside his tepee one sunny morn-ing. There had been no snowfall for almost two weeks, and much of the ground lay bare, promising the change of season that even so was still several weeks away. Young Horse came riding into the village amid frantic excitement, declaring to all that a small herd of buffalo had been sighted, and everyone must take advantage of this discovery.

'Quickly Munro! Saddle your horse and bring along that English rifle. We are going to hunt buffalo together.'

Suddenly the whole village became a hive of activity. Men and youths ran about securing the horses to be used in the hunt, while others gathered together the weapons to be used. The word had been got out that the hunters were to use traditional methods of bow and arrows, thus saving what gunpowder they possessed. Race, of course, was excluded from this decree.

Women, aided and hindered by the efforts of children, were busy creating travois upon which would be placed the butchered results of the hunt, and knives were honed in anticipation of the work in which they would be employed. Finally all were ready, and the long column moved out under the direction of Young Horse and the other hunting braves.

The buffalo herd, about thirty or forty strong, was to be found in a small valley three miles from the village. The Lakota silently gathered at the entrance to the valley, and Young Horse stationed the braves, including Munro, in a loose arc – then they advanced into the valley while the women waited for the killing to begin.

The arc of warriors slowly moved forwards, each brave carrying his bow in his left hand with an arrow notched and ready in the bowstring. Race had drawn his Snider from its saddle sheath, and having loaded, rode with the weapon across his saddle bow, holding the weapon at the small of the butt.

Initially the buffalo grazed totally unconcerned by the wall of death moving closer. Then an old bull lifted his shaggy head, and peering at the strange shapes approaching, discerned that all was not right. He turned and broke into a gentle canter, which rapidly became a gallop, and was immediately followed by the remainder of the herd – and away they thundered, bulls and cows and small calves desperately trying to keep up with the adults.

With the first indication of alarm by the old bull, Young Horse signalled the Lakota to move in for the kill, and each brave, drawing back his bowstring and guiding his horse with his knees, moved swiftly to close in upon his first victim. Riding alongside the buffalo the brave would let loose his arrow, aiming just behind the shoulder, then he would quickly reload to place a second arrow in that first buffalo or to select a second target.

Race, caught up in the excitement of the chase, spurred his horse to move up alongside a ton of swiftly moving buffalo, and gripping tight with his knees as he had been taught in the riding school, placed the muzzle of his Snider at close range to the woolly hide and pulled the trigger.

The result was instantaneous. The buffalo's front legs buckled and it went down head over heels as Race quickly strove to move himself and his steed clear of the dying animal. He was successful, and after reloading, sought a second victim.

All over the valley Lakota braves were doing the same thing, and it looked as though the whole herd had been slaughtered. Already the women and children of the tribe were running forward and butchering the dead and dying animals, ripping out the liver and eating it raw. They swiftly skinned each animal, first removing the humps and tongues which were considered delicacies, and then skilfully dismembered the carcasses, arms steeped in gore to the elbows, and proceeded to load them on to the travois.

Race rode slowly from the valley, momentarily sickened by the apparent savagery that he was observing, but then rationalized the carnage with the realization that the Lakota were doing what they had always done to survive, particularly as they used practically the whole animal, and had far more justification in killing the buffalo than the white men who hunted purely for the hides, or those who were shooting for trophies.

He had not seen Rosebud among the squaws, but accepted that no doubt she was present among the butchers, and he wasn't sure of his reaction if he had seen her similarly blood splattered, as his white upbringing revolted against the concept. It was therefore with great relief that Race, riding into the Lakota village, found her tending a fire outside the large

145

tepee with the explanation that she had been chosen to remain behind and prepare food, rather than accompany the hunters.

For days after the hunt all in the village were active in treating their spoils in various ways. Buffalo hides were staked out on the ground and scraped to remove all traces of fat or meat, which could putrefy and spoil the hide as it was drying. Racks were built upon which were hung strips of buffalo meat to dry in the wind and sun. Some of these dried strips would later be used in the making of pemmican. Buffalo fat was being rendered down over open fires and would then be poured into clay storage pots to be used as the weeks passed, and in one corner of the camp the village bow maker was busy selecting buffalo sinews, which would be stretched and possibly split before being dried and cured to use as bow strings and the bindings of other tools.

Then one day Race was sitting talking to Sitting Bull, watching Rosebud as she worked on a piece of beautifully tanned leather that she was fashioning into a vest for him, when one of the Hunkpapa scouts approached and spoke to Sitting Bull. The chief thanked him for his report and sat quietly for a moment before turning and addressing Race.

'Munro, the brave who has just left has passed on a report that has come to us from Lakota in the place where the sun rises, and it concerns you. The enemy you were hunting has left the place known as the "hole in the wall" with two other men, and is believed to be heading this way.'

CHAPTER TWENTY-ONE

Bill Westerman – or as he now thought of himself, Bill Webber – had found himself actually enjoying the winter months spent at the outlaw hideout known as the 'hole in the wall'. He had always been a loner, even during the months during which he was in the NWMP, and being thrown together day after day with the same small group of men who, though outwardly affable, could turn savage over mere trifles, taught him a great deal about human nature and how to turn an incident to his own advantage.

Webber became known as a good-natured fella always ready to pour oil on troubled waters whenever a contentious issue arose. He was always ready to volunteer if a work party was needed to assist in any of the tasks that enabled the small, tight-knit community to run smoothly, and did his share of guard duty, without the perpetual grumbling expressed by the others, huddled up amid the rocks at the head of the pass, buffeted by wind, rain and snow, ensuring that all strangers were vetted before they gained entry to the 'hole'.

Fortunately he established a very good relationship with Amos Smith and Tom Warner, the other inhabitants of his soddy, and while revealing very little of his own true background, gained a pretty fair knowledge of the others. From Amos he learned that when the Britisher was twelve he had gone home one evening to find his mother unconscious and bleeding from a terrible beating that she had received from one of her 'gentlemen friends'. Before she died she revealed the name of her assailant. Amos had tracked the man down and when he was deep into his cups had cut his throat from ear to ear. His act raised a hue and cry against him, and he had stowed away on a ship to avoid the gallows.

Arriving in New York he had promptly joined up with one of the city's street gangs, and his path through the United States had been punctuated by crimes carried out in diverse locations. All this Webber learned from Amos himself, as he gradually acquired the ability to understand Smith's fractured English.

Tom Warner's story was far more prosaic. Working as a farmhand in Indiana he had had an affair with his employer's wife, and the two of them were caught by the irate husband in a compromising situation in the hay loft. Heated words had led to physical violence, and in the ensuing fight the farmer was killed, although Tom still maintained that it had been an accident.

He, however, had left the state one jump ahead of the local posse, and he knew that there was no going back to Indiana. He and Amos had teamed up in some southern border town, and they'd been together as partners for several years now. Curiously, the pair of them seemed to welcome Bill Webber, not merely as a third member of the soddy, but as a close companion, as the three of them spent the winter evenings yarning and planning imaginary exploits. In time some more literate inhabitant of the 'hole' described them as the 'Terrible Trio', and the nickname stuck.

One day when the three of them sauntered over to the main cabin for their evening meal they were all interested that several new chums had arrived to spend part of the winter in the 'hole'. The newcomers were bearded, wore dark clothing, and were visibly nervous, as their gun hands were always hovering close to their weapons.

They tended to keep to themselves, and the whole group tended to defer to one man who was obviously the leader, and who would fly into a fierce rage if crossed by any of the others.

'Calm down, Jesse! Frank ain't saying you are wrong!' was a frequent cry as some more reasonable member of the group attempted to placate their irate leader, who once more was at loggerheads with the man who was in fact his older brother.

Thus Bill Webber rapidly came to know that their fellow residents of the 'hole in the wall' included the outlaw brothers Jesse and Frank James. When not arguing the James gang seemed to spend most of their time playing cards and gambling, with large sums of money obtained from their bank and railroad raids.

The Terrible Trio, upon retiring to their soddy, expressed considerable envy at the way in which the James gang casually tossed around large sums of money, and decided that with the coming of spring the three of them would sally forth and do a little bank robbery themselves.

By engaging in casual conversation with members of the James group, and even on occasion with the temperamental leader himself, they gathered together some of the techniques that had been used successfully by the premier bank robbers in the country.

'Always case the job beforehand. Have someone go in and sketch a general outline of employees' positions, and if there is a guard on duty. Favourable times are just after opening or shortly before closing. If possible wear respectable, sober clothing this would put people off their guard. Have a man at the hitching rail with the horses engaged in some innocuous task, reading a letter or a newspaper, and not merely standing there, which would stick out like a choir girl in a bawdy house.'

The above and many other tips were gathered and shared by the trio in their soddy, and all three looked forward to the coming of spring, when they intended to put their new-found knowledge into practice.

Two weeks later the People's Bank in the little town of Prairie Dog was held up at nine thirty in the morning shortly after the doors had been unlocked. John Stinson, the cashier, was pistol whipped because he was tardy about carrying out the orders of the two masked men who carried out the robbery, and Henry Marks the local deputy was shot and mortally wounded by a third member of this gang who was tending the horses that were subsequently used in their getaway.

Marks, while still conscious, gave a good description of the man who shot him, stating that he was short and, when challenged, spoke a strange kind of English. The robbers got away with 27,000 dollars, and it wasn't known where they went after leaving Prairie Dog.

CHAPTER TWENTY-TWO

Race Munro, upon receiving the news about Westerman from Sitting Bull, knew that it was time to resume the chase, and started gathering his traps together. Then he had Rosebud question the Lakota brave who had brought the news, and thus received word that Westerman was not travelling alone, and that he and his companions had just robbed a bank.

Rosebud was reluctant to give Race the information that she had obtained. 'Oh, Race! Can you not forget this man you have been following? We are happy here together you and I, and I know that there is as much love in your heart for me as there is in mine for you!' And she clutched at his shirt and buried her head against his chest in the vain hope of swaying him from his intended course of action.

Race gently eased her away, and holding her by the upper arms, shook her gently. 'Rosebud, my precious one. There is nothing that I would rather do than stay here with you, but it is a question of my honour. I promised my chief, Colonel French, that I would find this murderer and bring him to justice or kill him, and I cannot break my word, even for you, my sweet.'

At Sitting Bull's bidding one of the braves brought Race's roan, and he swiftly had her saddled and all his gear stowed ready to sally forth. With pemmican packed away in one saddlebag and a full canteen, and with both Colt and Snider loaded, there seemed nothing left to do but say farewell – and this he did, first to Sitting Bull, then Young Horse and his other Lakota friends, and finally to Rosebud, with a fervent promise that they would be together again one day.

After Race had left the village, Sitting Bull called Young Horse to him. 'Take one other warrior and follow Munro. Keep a safe watch over him, but do not let him know, because he is a proud man. But one man against three is not good. You two will make the battle more equal.'

Race knew nothing of his two chaperons as he rode roughly south-east among the Montana hills. He knew that somewhere to the south was the Bozeman Trail, and he recalled the notion that Westerman might attempt to hook up with some Oregon-bound wagon train and be lost among all the other travellers.

It was with this concern in his mind that Race Munro rode down into a wide valley where nestled a typical small western town consisting of one unpaved main street lined with unpainted clapboard buildings all with the same weathered appearance, even though the odds were that they had been erected a mere two or three years before. He passed a livery stable with a large corral out back in which a dozen horses were contentedly grazing on a huge bale of hay.

There was a barber's shop complete with red-and-white striped pole, which reminded Race that he would enjoy a good civilized shave and hair-cut. Then there was a hardware store facing a large saloon where a sole employee was briskly sweeping away the mud on the boardwalk. He paused in his labours to give Race a salute, to which the would-be marshal replied with a nod and a grin.

There were several private dwellings scattered among the stores, and then a more solid building, which by means of a large sign across the front announced to the whole world that this was Jamestown City Bank.

It was a trifle early for much business to be going on – but no, wait! There were three horses at the hitching rail and a runt of a man nearby studying a sheet of newsprint. As Race approached, the man folded his paper and then, seeing the marshal's badge prominently displayed on Race's vest, uttered a strange cry of 'Blimey! A bleedin' peeler!' He dropped into a crouch and at the same time hauled a big Colt Dragoon revolver into view from under his long riding coat.

Race simultaneously drew his pistol and dropped over on to the rear side of the roan as the Dragoon bellowed and the ball clipped a neat half circle from the rim of his hat.

Keeping low, Amos Smith scuttled like a crab to the safety of the bank door, firing a wild shot over his shoulder and yelling a warning to his fellow bandits inside, as Race fired his first shot, which hit the wretched man in the buttocks as he vanished into the bank. All Race Munro heard as the small figure disappeared from view was a loud cry of anguish, and then there was silence.

Keeping the roan between himself and the bank building, Race retreated across the street to the corner of a building where in moderate safety he drew his Snider; then he slapped the horse on the hindquarters, sending it further down a side alley out of harm's way.

In the short time since the first shot had been fired, other townsfolk had appeared armed with a medley of weapons and demanding to know what was happening. Race introduced himself tersely and described to them what had happened, and his information as to the possible outlaws. Then, taking command, he spread them out, surrounding the bank building in a loose cordon to prevent the would-be bank robbers from escaping.

Shortly after arranging the positions of this self-appointed posse there was a single shot from inside the bank and the door burst open as a dishevelled figure brandishing a Smith and Wesson pistol dashed for safety across the street. Two shots from the bank in rapid succession threw him spreadeagled down into the dust, the pistol flying from his hand as he hit the ground and expired.

The abrupt departure of the one and only bank employee was an ongoing bone of contention between the Terrible Trio, not the least because prior to his bid to escape he had retrieved an overlooked pistol and had fired one .32 calibre round, which had struck Tom Warner in the left hand and partially disabled him.

'Curse you, Tom! Whatcha let him get away for?' bellowed Bill Webber staring at Tom, who was applying an improvised field dressing one-handed to his mangled member, and at Amos crouched on his knees and pawing at his perforated posterior.

'Don't come the heavy on me, Bill Webber! That little runt ruined everything by panicking outside when he could 'ave bluffed that marshal easily!' replied Tom Warner, dismayed that their operation was going so awry.

'You think so, do yer?' grated Webber. 'Do yer know who that marshal is? He's Race Munro an' he's bin huntin' me for months. I don't know about you fellas, but I'm going to shoot my way out now before that mob get really organized. Who's with me?' and he looked around at his erstwhile partners.

The other two looked at him and at each other, and reluctantly agreed that he had suggested the only possible course of action apart from surrendering, and that was out of the question. As they were busy reloading and summoning up their courage for the proposed dash for freedom, there came a cry from outside.

'Hello, you men in the bank! We've got you completely surrounded! There's no chance of escaping! Throw your guns out and then come out with your hands high. You'll get a fair trial, I promise!'

There was a short pause and a voice from inside the bank replied, 'We're comin' out Marshal!' Moments later the three men emerged with guns blazing, only to be met by a hail of gunfire from the townspeople.

Tom Warner was the first to fall, riddled with bullet wounds in both arms and legs and a death-dealing load of buckshot that smashed into his chest. Amos Smith fell on top of his buddy, dead from a head shot, and as he fell an opened razor dropped on to the boardwalk.

Bill Webber cleared the boardwalk in two leaps and then fell as Race Munro's .577 bullet slammed into his left shoulder. With one arm hanging uselessly he staggered to his feet and moved purposefully across the street to where Race waited with Colt pistol drawn and pointed towards the ground.

When the murderous deserter was about ten paces from his former comrade he made a supreme effort and tried to raise his Adams revolver hip high to fire it, and as he did so Race raised his own gun and triggered three rounds, all of which hit Bill Westerman plumb centre in the chest and drove him back to fall dying in the street.

CHAPTER TWENTY-THREE

Race obtained an affidavit from a judge residing in Jamestown that the man he had just shot was indeed a deserter wanted for murder, and although travelling under the name of Bill Webber, was in fact Bill Westerman, as proven by the words tattooed on his left arm, a practice of many of the men who served in the Union army during the late Civil War.

Armed with the legal proof of Westerman's death, Race Munro felt duty bound to head straight north for the Canadian border, even though his heart wanted to be with Rosebud.

He called in at Fort Benson, but that location had reverted to being the trading company that had loaned the premises to the US government. The army had gone, and with them Race's friend Major Carson. So he did not delay there, but continued his journey north.

Arriving at Fort McCloud, Race reported to Colonel French and submitted a detailed account of his exploits while in the USA. It was agreed that in the interests of good relations with the southern neighbour there would be no public notice of his role as an American peace officer.

Meanwhile, relations between the American government and the various northern tribes continued to deteriorate, and Race heard that the Hunkpapa were among the Lakota who had sworn that they would not be driven from the Black Hills. He was worried about Rosebud, but there was no means of contacting her, and he just had to hope that she was safe.

The months passed, and finally the news came north that the Sioux, as the Lakota were described by white sources, had won a great victory on 25 June 1876 over a large force of United States cavalry. Apparently about two hundred and sixty men of the 7th Cavalry and their commanding officer Colonel Custer had been trapped and killed in a battle described by the Lakota as the 'Battle of the Greasy Grass'.

More US troops were brought in columns to try and force the Lakota to surrender their freedom and settle down on government reservations, and gradually the action concentrated on a number of holdouts who refused to surrender.

Finally on 5 May 1877 Sitting Bull, with a small number of ragged and starving Hunkpapa men, women and children, crossed the border into Canadian territory and sought refuge in the land of the 'White Queen' (Victoria). With this band was a young Lakota woman who went by the name of Rosebud, and she shortly thereafter was reunited and married to a certain Sergeant Race Munro of the NWMP.